WITHERING
by
SEA

Withering by Sea

Judith Rossell

atheneum

ATHENEUM BOOKS FOR YOUNG READERS

New York London Toronto Sydney New Delhi

atheneum

ATHENEUM BOOKS FOR YOUNG READERS
An imprint of Simon & Schuster Children's Publishing Division
1230 Avenue of the Americas, New York, New York 10020

The verse on page 64 is from *Divine Songs for Children*, Number 10, "Solemn thoughts of God and Death," in *Divine Songs Attempted in Easy Language for the Use of Children* by Isaac Watts, first published 1715.
The verse on page 112 is from the song "Married to a Mermaid," by James Thompson (1700–1748) and David Mallet (1705–1765).

Book design by Debra Sfetsios-Conover
The text for this book is set in Adobe Jenson Pro.
The illustrations for this book are rendered in ink, pencil, water color, and digital work.
Manufactured in the United States of America
0216 FFG
First US Edition
10 9 8 7 6 5 4 3 2 1
Library of Congress Cataloging-in-Publication Data
Rossell, Judith.
Withering-by-Sea / Judith Rossell. — First US edition.
pages cm
Originally published: Australia : HarperCollins Publishers Australia Pty Limited, 2014.
ISBN 978-1-4814-4367-8 (hardcover) — ISBN 978-1-4814-4369-2 (eBook)
[1. Adventure and adventurers—Fiction. 2. Magic—Fiction. 3. Identity—Fiction. 4. Orphans—Fiction. 5. Aunts—Fiction. 6. Hotels, motels, etc.—Fiction. 7. Mystery and detective stories.] I. Title. PZ7.R719983Wit 2016
[Fic]—dc23 2015002051

For Hazel, Spider, Mouse, and Myn

One

Stella Montgomery lay hidden behind the ferns in the conservatory of the Hotel Majestic, flat on the mossy tiles, tracing a path through the Amazon jungle in a small, damp atlas. She skirted around a vague outcrop of some kind—possibly mildew—and continued upriver. The drip and trickle of water and the hiss of steam under the grating in the floor seemed to mingle with the swish of jungle trees in the wind and the screams of parrots. Stella wiped some water drops off the map and read, *On the trees, thousands of curious and gorgeous orchids live and flower*. The jungle was full of all kinds of dangers—vampire bats, earthquakes, and hunters armed with blowpipes full of poison darts.

Serpents forty feet long and capable of swallowing considerable quadrupeds, such as hares, goats, deer &c.

There was a picture of such a serpent in the margin. Stella studied it wistfully. It looked large enough to swallow an elephant, and had a hungry expression. A serpent of that size could swallow a person, an Aunt for example, as easy as kiss your hand. Several Aunts, probably. It looked sufficiently hungry. The people who lived in the Amazon jungle would not be bothered by Aunts.

After eating, they lie torpid for several weeks. Stella imagined the enormous serpent sleeping off a dinner of three Aunts. Aunt Condolence for starters, Aunt Temperance for next, and then Aunt Deliverance for pudding. There would be three big lumps in the sleeping serpent.

She picked up the second of her stolen apples and took a bite. It was small, green, hard, and sour. She chewed grimly and headed upstream toward the silver mines of the Andes, the calls of monkeys ringing in her ears, jaguars lurking in the undergrowth, and toucans flying overhead.

Sudden footsteps clattered on the grating near the fountain, close to where she was lying. With a slight jolt, she returned from the Amazon, back into what could be real danger. Right now, at this moment, she should be upstairs in the Aunts' parlor, learning a lesson from *French Conversation for Young Ladies,* and instead she was doing at least four forbidden things, all at once.

Stella kept one finger on the Amazon River and peered through the ferns to get a glimpse of the intruder, but all she could see were dripping green leaves.

In the late morning the conservatory was usually empty. The hotel servants were busy in the kitchen and the bathhouse. The hotel residents, including all three Aunts, should be in the bathhouse, or wrapped up and propped in cane chairs in the long sunroom, sipping glasses of murky water. (Stella had tasted the water once. It tasted exactly as it smelled, as if rusty nails and bad eggs had been boiled up in a puddle. It came right out of the ground, from an ancient spring underneath the hotel. The water was what made the Hotel Majestic famous. People came from all over the country to drink it. It was hard to believe, but it was true.)

She gave a silent sigh of relief to see that the intruder wasn't an Aunt. It was Mr. Filbert, an elderly foreign gentleman. He was a new resident. He had been at the hotel only a few days.

Stella liked him. He was small and frail, almost insubstantial. His voice was whispery, like rustling leaves, and his manners were old-fashioned. Every morning he bowed to Stella from across the breakfast room. His eyes were twinkling and alert, but his skin was pale, almost greenish, and stretched tightly across the bones of his face. Like many of the residents at the Hotel Majestic, he appeared to be rather unwell. However, he drank the water every day and it seemed to be doing him good.

Mr. Filbert had caused somewhat of a sensation during luncheon on his first day. He had pushed away his plate of mutton-in-aspic and had asked for greens. Then he had opened a small leather bag and sprinkled a pinch of brown powder over the boiled spinach, with flickering fingers. An earthy smell had drifted across the dining room, causing much muttering and tut-tutting amongst the other residents.

General Carruthers had grunted in a military manner and then marched from the dining room without having any pudding. After luncheon, Stella had seen him stamping around the garden, despite the icy wind, shouting at the wintry flower beds. Foreigners always made the general bad-tempered. Stella supposed this was because he had spent so much of his life fighting wars with them.

Now Mr. Filbert seemed nervous. Stella silently sank farther behind the ferns. Mr. Filbert's twig-like fingers twisted together. He hesitantly walked toward the enormous Chinese urn that stood just beyond where Stella was hiding. It was planted with a drooping, feathery fern. He pushed aside some of the fronds and prodded his fingers into the soil. He shot a furtive look over his shoulder. Then he darted his hand into his inside coat pocket and brought out a small packet. He held it tightly for a moment, and then pushed it down in amongst the roots of the fern and pressed soil over it. He let the fronds fall back into place. He turned on his heel, dipped his fingers into the fountain, and hurried away, wiping his hands with his handkerchief as he went.

As his footsteps died away, Stella found she had been holding her breath. She let it out. She waited a moment and then got up and walked softly around the path to the urn. It was very tall. Stella pushed the fern fronds aside and stood on tiptoe to feel around in the soil. What could he be hiding that made him so nervous? Perhaps he had Aunts of his own, she thought sympathetically.

Her fingers dug into the damp soil, but before she found the little package, the door handle rattled and brisk footsteps came along the tiled path. Stella jumped back from the urn, stumbling over her feet. She turned, expecting to see Mr. Filbert again, but it was Ada, Aunt Deliverance's maid. She looked sharp-eyed and annoyed.

"There you are, miss." Ada strode briskly past the fountain and stood, hands on hips, her lips tight and sour-looking. "I knew you'd be skriving somewhere. Always hiding, you are. And where were you at luncheon?"

"Luncheon?" Stella hadn't realized how much time had passed in the Amazon. And now she'd missed luncheon. The Aunts would be seething.

"As if I don't have better things to do than play hidey seek all the time. Come on." She took Stella's arm in a hard grip. "Look at you. All over with slime. Making more work for people." Ada flicked an angry hand at the green streaks on the front of Stella's pinafore and marched out of the conservatory, gripping Stella's arm so tightly and walking so briskly that she was half dragged along. She had to jog every few steps to keep up.

"I can walk myself," Stella said, halfway down the empty morning room.

"Hush. You're two people's work, you are."

The afternoon sunshine through the windows of the long sunroom made colored shapes on the floor and on the residents, who sat in cane chairs, sipping the water. Stella blinked. Overhead, the steam pipes hissed and clanked. The residents who had come from the wave bath or the steam bath emitted little curling wisps of vapor. The ones from the plunge bath were a shiny pink, and those from the ice bath were shivering and gasping.

A mumbled chorus of disapproval accompanied Ada and Stella's progress along the room. Several elderly ladies pursed their lips. Colonel Fforbes made a tut-tutting noise, and so did his ancient macaw, Wellington. Lady Clottington muttered something and tucked her feet under her chair as Stella passed, as if she were contagious. Sir Oswald, Lady Clottington's bad-tempered little dog, dashed out from under a small table and snapped at Stella's ankles. Despite his gout, he was as quick as a weasel, but Ada whisked Stella past, and there was a sharp click of walrus ivory as the dog's false teeth shut on nothing.

In the entrance hall, new residents were arriving: a tall man and a thin, pale boy. The man wore black; he had a narrow yellowish face and green-tinted spectacles. He turned to look at them, but Ada did not slow down. The man's intent gaze followed them.

As they approached the Vertical Omnibus it was clear that James, the conductor, was busy with the new residents. So Stella followed Ada's scolding voice all the long way up the winding back stairs.

In Stella's tiny bedroom, Ada continued scolding in an undertone as she snatched off Stella's soggy pinafore and pushed her firmly into a stiff, clean one, tying the strings with angry little jerks. She said, "Hold still, drat you, miss," as she pulled the hairbrush through Stella's wispy, mouse-colored hair.

"I'm sorry, Ada," said Stella, and she sniffed.

"Yes, well," said Ada. She tied Stella's hair back with a new ribbon and gave her an awkward pat on the top of her head. She said, "Change your stockings. Put on your slippers. Wash your hands and face." Then she pointed toward the parlor door and told her if she knew what was good for her, she'd buckle down to it.

Stella thought of the enormous serpent, sleeping

in the Amazon jungle, full of Aunts. That should have cheered her up, but it did not. This was not the Amazon jungle. That was far away, on the other side of the world. This was the Hotel Majestic, and there were no giant serpents here.

Nothing ever happened here at all.

Two

The Hotel Majestic stood high on a cliff, overlooking the town of Withering-by-Sea. It was enormous and white and had towers and turrets and curlicues and columns and chimneys and balconies and lots of curly metal sprouting here and there. It looked like a gigantic marzipan wedding cake.

The Aunts, as long-term residents, occupied some of the best rooms on the third floor, with a view of the sea, the lighthouse, and the marsh beyond the town. They had a parlor with a pianoforte, a drawing room, two large bedrooms, and a private bathroom. Stella's room was not much bigger than a cupboard. It was really a dressing room, and to get to it she had to pass through the large bedroom that Aunt Condolence and Aunt Temperance

shared. Ada slept in the tiny dressing room of Aunt Deliverance's bedroom, which was on the other side of the parlor.

Aunt Deliverance was confined to a wheeled bath chair and spent much of her time in the bathhouse undergoing treatments, so Stella saw her only at mealtimes and for the daily promenade along the Front, and that was more than enough. She saw Aunt Condolence and Aunt Temperance for her lessons. (Pianoforte, Deportment, Needlework, and French, and Stella could not have said which she hated most.)

Half an hour later, after a brisk, unpleasant scolding from Aunt Temperance, Stella sat stiffly at the parlor table and struggled to learn a list of French phrases to say to the wife of a bishop whilst drinking tea. (*It wants but ten minutes to three o'clock. Is this not dreadful weather? I am delighted to see you in such tolerable health.*) She suddenly remembered the Atlas. Instead of hiding it carefully in the biscuit tin underneath the ferns, she had left it lying open in the middle of the path, where anyone walking around the conservatory might stumble upon it. Her sharp indrawn breath made Aunt Temperance look up from her embroidery and say, "Quiet, child!"

Stella looked down at *French Conversation for Young*

Ladies again (*The pattern of this carpet is exceedingly vulgar*), chewed her lip, and tried to decide what to do. The Atlas had belonged to Dr. Frobisher, an African explorer who had stayed at the hotel for several months with jungle fever, sleeping sickness, scurvy, and malaria. After he had died, his room had been fumigated with burning brimstone and Stella had found the Atlas on a rubbish heap, only slightly charred. It had been lying amongst bundles of letters, broken strings of colored glass beads, and several wooden figures, which Aunt Deliverance would have said were shockingly vulgar, had she seen them. Stella had rescued it and kept it hidden. It was her greatest treasure, and any minute it might be discovered.

Without lifting her head from *French Conversation for Young Ladies*, she looked out of the corner of her eye. Aunt Temperance was sitting, bony and upright, by the window, sewing a pattern of violets in immaculate stitches onto an antimacassar. As usual, while one of her watery eyes was fixed on her work, the other's attention seemed to be roving here and there around the room in a disconcerting manner, like a marble rolling around in an eggcup. She seemed very alert. Stella sighed, and looked back down at the book. (*It is not likely that this rain will cease. You are too kind. Permit me to offer you some cake.*)

The afternoon dragged on. The clock on the mantelpiece ticked, and sometimes a seagull cried as it sailed past the window.

Aunt Temperance said, "Don't swing your legs like that, child," and twenty minutes later, "Don't slouch. Sit up straight."

Stella tried to concentrate. She fixed her eyes on her lesson book (*The mists that rise from the marshes are injurious to the constitution*) but her thoughts kept returning to the Atlas, lying open in the conservatory, three stories below.

Time passed slowly.

At last teatime arrived. Aunt Deliverance rolled majestically into the parlor, like an enormous boiled pudding, in her wickerwork bath chair. Ada pushed the bath chair, and Aunt Condolence waddled behind. Aunt Condolence was very short and extremely wide. She wore a Particular Patent Corset of springs and whalebone, which creaked and twanged as she moved.

Two parlormaids followed with tea on silver trays. There was a cake stand, with thin bread and butter cut into little triangles, coconut macaroons, and seedcake. While Aunt Condolence poured the tea and Ada passed the cups, Aunt Deliverance asked, "Has the child been dutiful and diligent?" Her black eyes were fixed disapprovingly on Stella. "After her appalling behavior this morning?"

"She has, on the whole, sister," replied Aunt Temperance.

"Shocking behavior," said Aunt Condolence. Her Particular Patent Corset gave an outraged twang. "Always creeping around and hiding. Disgraceful, even for a half—"

"Quiet, sister!" snapped Aunt Deliverance, looking thunderous.

Aunt Condolence shut her mouth with a snap.

Stella thought, *A half what?*

Aunt Deliverance glared at Aunt Condolence, and then at Stella, took a sip of tea, and said, "Well, shall we hear her lesson?" To Stella she said, "Bring me your book, if you please, child. I trust you were not daydreaming yet again."

With a sinking feeling, Stella realized she had

been thinking mainly about the Atlas, and then she had spent some more time thinking about the enormous Aunt-eating serpent, and some of the other dangers lurking in the Amazon jungle. She looked longingly at the cake stand. She had eaten only those two little green apples since breakfast time, and she was hungry.

But it was very difficult to remember the exact words. They seemed to get tangled inside her head. She twisted her fingers together behind her back, took a breath, and said, in tolerable French, "I am delighted to see you in such dreadful health, Aunt Deliverance. You are exceedingly vulgar. Permit me to offer you some carpet."

Stella lay facedown on her bed, in her nightgown, in the dark, in disgrace. She heard the Aunts go down for dinner. She slept for several hours and then woke to hear the twangs and creaks and little gasping yelps as Aunt Temperance helped Aunt Condolence loosen her Particular Patent Corset. Then there were murmured voices, taps and clinks and creaks of bedsprings and then, at last, snores. Whining snores from Aunt Temperance, piglike grunts from Aunt Condolence, and more distant, booming snores from Aunt Deliverance's bedroom, which was on the other side of the parlor.

Stella sighed miserably and rolled over onto her back. No luncheon, no tea, and no dinner. Her stomach made a hungry noise. She got up from her bed and silently tried the door handle. It was locked. She went to the window, pushed back the thick curtains, heaved open the window, and looked out at the night. There were no stars, but gaslights glowed along the Front, and distant tinny music drifted up from the pier. Stella leaned on the windowsill, breathed the cold air, and thought about the Atlas, lying open in the conservatory. It would certainly be discovered in the morning when the gardener came in to water the ferns. And that would be the end of her beautiful Atlas, and her only book would be *French Conversation for Young Ladies,* forever and ever.

Just outside her window was a wide, flat ledge. Perhaps a foot wide. It went along past the window of Aunt Temperance and Aunt Condolence's bedroom, and that window was also open. (Aunt Temperance believed that fresh air at night was healthy.) Stella touched the ledge with one finger. There were little patches of lichen and bird droppings, but not enough to make it slippery. To walk along the ledge would really be no different from walking along a footpath. Stella had often thought how easy it would be. Particularly if she didn't look down. It would be only a few steps to the Aunts' bedroom window. And if she was going to do it, she should do it now, while the Aunts were sound asleep.

She pushed the window up farther and leaned out. A few lights from the hotel windows reflected onto the paved patio, three stories below. It was deserted, apart from the stone lions, and it looked extremely hard. Stella swallowed.

But she fixed her thoughts on the Atlas. *In the perilous heights of the Himalayas, the sure-footed yak bounds safely amongst the loftiest crags.* She stood on tiptoe, got one knee onto the sill, and pulled herself out of the window. Gripping the window frame tightly, she knelt upon the sill, facing back into her bedroom. She tried to ignore the way her insides seemed to be quivering coldly.

"Just like a footpath," she muttered, and pulled herself to her feet. The ledge didn't seem quite as wide as she had thought, but the surface felt slightly rough under her bare feet, which made it easy to grip. Right beside the window was a stone lady's head.

Stella ignored the dizzying feeling of empty space dropping away behind her. She reached out and took hold of the lady's nose. Keeping her face against the wall, she took her first step along the ledge, sideways like a crab. Beyond the lady's head there were some curly stone flowers. She gripped them, edged another step along, and then another.

Just before the Aunts' window was another stone lady's head; this one seemed to be faintly smiling. Two more steps and Stella had one hand on the lady's chin and the other on the Aunts' window frame. As carefully as she could, she lowered herself to her knees again, and then down to a sitting position, and poked her legs through the open window into the Aunts' bedroom. She felt around with her feet and found the edge of the embroidered ottoman that lived just beside the window. She planted both feet firmly and slithered down into the room. She landed on the ottoman with a soft thump, letting out her breath in a silent, shuddering gasp.

Both Aunts were still snoring. Stella could just make out Aunt Temperance's long, bony shape in one bed and Aunt Condolence's hippopotamus shape in the other. She tiptoed between the beds to the door. As she passed, Aunt Condolence gave a grunt and turned over. Stella jumped and made a tiny, startled sound. She pressed her hand to her mouth. But Aunt Condolence settled down, snuffled, and started her piglike snoring again almost immediately. Stella crept across the room to the parlor door, opened it, and glided through, as silent as a cat.

Three

The Hotel Majestic was quite different at night. The gas was turned low, so there were dark shadows in doorways and corners. Indistinct voices and other sounds echoed in the stairwells. Stella crept along the passageway and started down the winding back stairs. On the first landing she froze. Two maids were below. One was sitting on a step, leaning against the banister with her back to Stella. The other lolled on a wooden chair with her feet up. Stella ducked down and peered around the banister. They were sleeping. Could she creep past without waking them? It seemed unlikely. She turned and tiptoed back up the stairs and along the deserted passageway to the main staircase.

Gas hissed in the big rounded lamps and in the gigantic dangling chandelier. The brightness made

Stella blink. She leaned over to see, three floors below, the marble floor of the entrance hall, and the shiny bald head of the night manager, Mr. Blenkinsop. He was slumped across his desk and he, too, seemed to be asleep.

She tiptoed down two flights of stairs, keeping close to the wall in case Mr. Blenkinsop should happen to glance up. The stair carpet was soft and silent underfoot, and the marble on the landings was very cold and smooth. *The pattern of this carpet is exceedingly vulgar.* She stifled a giggle, ducked down a side passageway, and slipped into the library.

The library was shadowy and full of obstacles. Stella crept between the awkward high-backed chairs and statues of gentlemen's heads on alabaster pillars. A loud snort made her stiffen. She peered around the back of a chair. It was General Carruthers. He smacked his lips together twice and started to snore. Everyone in the hotel seemed to be sleeping. *Except for me,* thought Stella.

Beside the sleeping general, on a carved table in the shape of an elephant, rested a glass of brandy and three square biscuits on a little plate. Stella's stomach growled like a hungry jaguar.

She tiptoed over to a small door at the far side

of the library, slipped through it, and crept down a narrow staircase and into the dark sunroom. The only sounds were her teeth munching the general's biscuits (this sounded extremely loud inside her head; the general's biscuits came by sea from Scotland and they were very hard), her soft footfalls, and the occasional hiss and clank from the steam pipes.

In the sunroom, she threaded her way between cane chairs and aspidistras in brass jars. The morning room beyond was very dark. She crossed it silently. She pushed open the door to the conservatory and slipped inside. The ferns were dark, banking shadows on either side of the pale tiled path. Water dripped and steam hissed under the gratings in the floor. She tiptoed past the silent fountain and followed the path behind the Chinese urn.

And there, lying just as she had left it, was the Atlas. Stella gave a gasp of relief, snatched it up, and hugged it to her chest. It was even damper than usual and it smelled of moss, but it was safe.

Then she remembered Mr. Filbert's strange behavior earlier that day, and how he had hidden the tiny package in the Chinese urn. Was it still there? She followed the path around to the urn, parted the drooping fern fronds, stood on tiptoe, and reached up. She dug into the earth with her fingers, felt the package among the roots of the fern, and pulled it out. It was small. She could hold it easily in one hand. It was too dark to see clearly, but it felt as though it was wrapped in oil-cloth and tied with string. What could it be?

She reached up to put the little package safely back into its hiding place, but then froze, her heart thumping. She heard a crash from somewhere nearby. Then footsteps and raised voices. Clutching the Atlas and Mr. Filbert's package, she crept to the door of the conservatory, pushed it open an inch, put her eye to the crack, and peered out into the darkness. The door on the far side of the morning room had a colored glass window in it, and she could see a light flickering red and blue.

Crash. The door banged open, and an enormous man stamped into the morning room. He held a candlestick with three flaring candles in a hand that looked like a bunch of sausages. He turned, and Stella stifled a gasp. For a horrible moment she thought he had the face, the protruding snout, of an animal. But then she saw he wore a buckled leather mask that covered his nose and mouth. He shoved it up onto his forehead, wiped a hand over his mouth, spat, and said, "Tastes like a flippin' grunter's ken, don't it, Scuttler."

"Pipe down, Charlie." A smaller man, also wearing a mask, slunk into the room. The mask made his voice sound distant and grating. His eyes darted around furtively. He had pale whiskers and wore a cerulean waistcoat with a pattern of roses.

The first man laughed. "It don't matter, Scuttler. The Professor's got the bleedin' hand o' glory, ain't he?" He laughed again nervously and glanced back over his shoulder.

"That thing gives me chills, Charlie," said the second man. "And it don't feel very professional-like, making all this rumbo. Put your gasper back on, mate, you don't want to be nodding off."

The big man shrugged and pushed the mask back over his nose and mouth. He put the candlestick on a low table, overturned a chair, and probed its underside with his enormous fingers. "Just a tiny, niggle thing, and hid somewhere. But a bleedin' golden strike to him as finds it." With the mask on, his voice was muffled and metallic.

Thieves. Searching for something. Stella let the conservatory door close softly, scurried into a dark patch of shadow behind a big fern, and crouched there. She tightened her grip on the Atlas and Mr. Filbert's package as the crashes and thumps came closer.

Footsteps approached and the door handle rattled. The second man pushed open the door. "Charlie, there's a flippin' great greenhouse in here. Bring that glimstick."

The big man elbowed his way through the door. Candlelight flickered and reflected off the wet ferns and the glass panes in the walls and roof. Stella held her breath. Above his mask, the smaller man's eyes were alert and sharp. She was sure he would see her. For a moment she felt dizzy and strange. As if she were somehow fading away, to become part of the shadow. Her head swam. The man's gaze slid over her without pausing. As he turned away, Stella let out a cautious, silent breath. She had always been extremely good at hiding.

"It's a bleedin' jungle, Charlie." The big man started down the path toward the fountain, holding the candlestick high and looking about. The candle flames scuttered and flared, making his enormous shadow loom and flicker.

After a darting glance all around, the smaller man followed him. They moved past Stella, almost close enough for her to touch, and then away down the path. She watched them circling the fountain.

The big man kicked over a flowerpot with a crash, and both men laughed. They had their backs to her.

Stella started to creep from her hiding place.

A soft voice spoke from just above her.

"Gentlemen," said the voice. It wasn't loud, but something about it made Stella shiver. She covered her mouth with a trembling hand and shrank back into the shadow, her heart thumping.

The two men stopped laughing immediately and came back along the path. "Professor," they muttered.

A tall man stepped into Stella's view. A gaunt shadow, silhouetted against the flickering candle-light. One pale hand rested on the head of a cane with a handle shaped like a serpent's head. On one finger was a ring with a dark stone. It glittered red in the light of the candles. Stella recognized the man. He was the new resident she had seen in the entrance hall. She remembered his thin, yellowish face, green spectacles, and steady, intent gaze.

Several masked figures followed him into the conservatory, carrying candles. Two of the men half carried, half dragged a limp body between them. But it was the tall man who drew Stella's attention. There was something compelling about him, although he was very still and spoke quietly. Stella's fingernails dug into her palms.

He gestured with his cane, and the masked men dragged the body forward and dropped it onto the floor. As the candlelight caught its face, Stella recognized Mr. Filbert. He lay sprawled, his head lolling. His eyes were closed, and a thin line of blood trickled from one ear and stained his shirt collar. He was dressed only in shirt and trousers and he had slippers on his feet, as if he had been getting ready for bed.

The Professor said, "Our friend here has not been as forthcoming as I would wish. But I have extracted something. It seems my property is concealed here." He gestured with his long, pale fingers. "But where, exactly, I wonder?" He looked down at Mr. Filbert. "I could have my men tear this place apart. But I would not be certain of finding it, would I? And there is an easier way."

Mr. Filbert's eyelids flickered and his eyes opened. He took a breath with obvious effort and said, "I will never tell you, I . . ."

His voice trailed off as the Professor said, "No, Dryad, perhaps not. But there is, as I mentioned, an easier way." He gestured again, and a small figure was pushed into the candlelight.

It was the thin, pale boy Stella had seen in the entrance hall. The Professor beckoned, and the boy shook his head but took two steps forward. He said, "No, no. Please, sir," in a low voice.

The Professor passed his cane to one of the masked men, placed a hand on the boy's shoulder, and pulled him closer. The gesture looked gentle, but the boy winced.

"Hold out your hands." The Professor turned the ring on his finger, and the dark stone caught the light and gleamed.

The boy's eyes were on the ring. He looked as if he might cry. He shook his head again but obeyed, cupping his hands together. His fingers and palms were stained black. The man took a small bottle of ink from his coat pocket, unscrewed the lid, and poured the ink into the boy's cupped, trembling hands. He recapped the bottle and returned it to his pocket. Then he placed one hand on the boy's unwilling head and tilted it forward, until the boy was forced to stare into the pool of ink he held in his hands.

"See," said the Professor.

The boy stopped trembling and stood stiff, his eyes quite empty.

"I see," he said.

Four

The boy's pale face was quite blank as he gazed into the pool of ink he held in his cupped hands.

"Do you see him?" asked the Professor. Candlelight glinted off his spectacles, turning the lenses into flickering yellow disks.

"I see him," answered the boy. His voice was expressionless.

"Do you see him hiding something?"

"I see him hiding a little thing," said the boy.

"Can you show me where?"

"I can."

The Professor removed his hand from the boy's head. The boy stumbled backward. Ink spilled from his hands. He bent over, gasping and coughing.

"Come on, boy." The Professor licked his lips. "Where is it?"

The boy pointed, his ink-stained fingers shaking. "Down there, sir. In that big pot."

The Professor took his cane, turned, and strode toward the fountain. The masked men followed, pulling the boy with them. Stella watched them move away, and then glanced down at Mr. Filbert, lying forgotten on the tiles.

She almost cried out in surprise. His eyes were open, and he was looking straight at her. With an effort, he raised his finger to his lips.

Stella nodded, her heart thumping. She opened her hand to reveal the package. She started to explain why she taken it, but he whispered quickly, "Hide it. Keep it safe."

There was a shout and an enormous crash from the other end of the conservatory. The Chinese urn lay smashed on the tiled path. Two of the masked men dropped to their knees and scrabbled amongst the broken pieces.

"Go, go, child," whispered Mr. Filbert. He raised himself up on one elbow. "Go now. Hide it. Keep it safe. Promise me."

Stella nodded. "I will."

"Remember . . ." He started to say something more, but then he collapsed and his eyes closed.

Stella crept out of her hiding place.

One of the masked men searching through the smashed pieces of the Chinese urn said something, looked up at the Professor, and shrugged. The Professor raised his cane and struck him hard on the side of his head, and he fell to the ground.

Stella bent and touched Mr. Filbert's cheek. His skin felt rough, like the bark of a tree. He did not move.

One of the men shouted something.

Stella jumped to her feet.

"Look! A nipper!"

Stella turned and ran.

There were shouts and crashes behind her. She sprinted through the morning room, her bare feet silent, clutching the Atlas and Mr. Filbert's package to her chest. She darted around an overturned chair and banged through the door into the sunroom. She paused for a fraction of a second. She could hear voices behind, and see candlelight flickering. She then turned and slipped through the small door to the servants' passageway. She ran along the passageway and up the stairs, two at a time.

In the library the lights were burning dimly, and the air felt thick and still. The general snored in his chair.

"General Carruthers," gasped Stella. She pulled his arm. It flopped off the armrest and dangled. Stella clutched it and shook it. "General!" she called, as loudly as she dared. She thumped his shoulder. "General! Please. Wake up. There are thieves, and . . ." She walloped his chest with her fist. The general made a grunting noise, but then started to snore again.

Stella picked up the glass from the little table and threw the drink in the general's face. He snorted in his sleep and smacked his lips together. Brandy dripped off his whiskers.

"General!" she shouted, louder than she wanted to. But he slept on.

Crash. It sounded as if someone was smashing furniture in the sunroom. There was a loud laugh, a door slammed, and footsteps started clumping up the stairs. Where could she hide?

The door banged open.

She flung herself down and squeezed underneath the general's chair. The metal springs poked into her back, but she wriggled her way underneath with determination and folded her legs up. Her face pressed into the dusty carpet. She hoped she would not sneeze.

A voice said, loud and close, "I reckon you were mistook, Charlie. You're seeing things. And now the Professor's in a right maggoty flummox."

A second voice said, "It was a nipper, Scuttler. I'm dead certain."

"Like when you were dead certain you seen that headless hound? Out on the marsh when we were cutting down that blasted tree? Scared the flippin' innards out of me, that did."

"It was bent around, Scuttler."

"A fair difference between a headless hound and a barker bent around having an old scratch, Charlie."

"I know what I seen."

Stella held her breath and listened to the tramping feet and the creaks and thumps as the men searched the room. Above her, the general snored. Stella hoped that they wouldn't think to look under his chair.

The first voice said, "Any nipper'd be snoozing, like old puff-guts there, anyhow. What with the Professor's hand o' glory alight."

"That thing gives me the right shudders, Scuttler."

"Me too, Charlie. Me too."

He said something that Stella didn't catch, and there was an enormous crash. She jumped and a chair spring jabbed into her back.

There were a few more scuffling noises and thumps and one of the men said, "Well, there ain't no nippers in here, Charlie."

A door handle rattled, a door opened, and the footsteps clumped away. Stella let out a cautious, silent breath. She waited a minute or two and then wriggled out from under the chair. She tiptoed over the smashed pieces of an alabaster pillar and peered out the door. The passageway was empty. The men had gone.

She slipped out of the library and crept along to the main staircase.

The big round lights flickered and hissed. The air seemed waxy and heavy. There was nobody in sight. Stella peered over the banister rail. Down in the entrance hall, Mr. Blenkinsop lay slumped across his desk, sound asleep. Stella tiptoed down the stairs.

"Mr. Blenkinsop," she whispered. "Wake up! Thieves!" She jerked his arm. He slipped off the desk and flopped sideways in his chair. His head lolled back and his mouth opened, but he did not wake up.

"Mr. Blenkinsop!" Stella shook his arm again and then hit him as hard as she could, somewhere in his middle. He snorted in his sleep and then he began to snore. Stella felt like screaming. Why wouldn't he wake up? This wasn't normal sleeping. She looked around desperately.

She froze. She felt her insides turn over.

The table just inside the big front doors usually held a china vase in the shape of a swan, filled with flowers. Now the vase lay smashed in a puddle of water, the flowers scattered across the floor. And in its place—Stella took two steps closer.

It was a hand. It stood upright on its wrist in a silver stand. It was black and twisted, with long, hornlike nails. At the tip of each finger a pale candle flame burned steadily. Tendrils of thin black smoke snaked upward, curling into the air.

She felt the back of her neck prickle. This must be the hand of glory the thieves had talked about. It had sounded extremely sinister, and it certainly looked revolting. Somehow, it was making everyone stay asleep. It must be the smoke. It was filling the air with a thick, drowsy haze.

She picked her way carefully closer. She could feel her heart beating in her ears.

She blew hard at the candle flames. They didn't flicker. She licked her fingertips, as she had seen Ada do hundreds of times to snuff out a candle, but she couldn't bring herself to touch the horrible thing. She clamped her teeth together, lifted the Atlas, and swatted the hand off the table. It toppled into the puddle. The fingers writhed and twisted, and the five pale flames spat and hissed.

There was a crash from upstairs. Voices and footsteps approached. At any moment she would be discovered.

Desperately, Stella stamped on the squirming, sputtering hand. It wriggled under her bare foot. She

felt the scorching flames and the scratching, horrible fingernails. It stung. She yelped. Blood oozed into the puddle underfoot, making red, watery trails.

One of the flames sizzled and went out.

Footsteps started down the staircase.

Stella stamped one more time on the hand. It clawed at her foot. Another flame went out with a hiss. She kicked at it and looked around, close to panic, for somewhere to hide. Beside the front door was the enormous carved mahogany umbrella stand. She scrambled over to it, crawled in behind the bristling jungle of walking sticks and umbrellas, and crouched down, her heart thumping.

Through a gap between a large black umbrella and an ebony walking stick, she could just see the hand lying in the puddle, sputtering and writhing, the three remaining pale flames making wiggly reflections in the water.

Several masked men came down the main staircase to the entrance hall.

With a horrible jolt in her stomach, Stella saw the trail of slightly bloody, wet footprints that she had left behind her. They led, like a line of arrows across the marble floor, right to where she was hiding.

Five

Stella watched the masked men. She could hear her heart thumping. In only a few moments they would see the footprints, and they would find her. She clutched the Atlas and Mr. Filbert's package, ready to run.

"Strike anything?" one of the men said.

"Nothin' at all. Just flash coves kipping."

"Flipping heck!" He pointed at the hand of glory where it lay in the puddle.

"Go on, Charlie, snabble it. It's going out."

"I ain't touching it. You nab it."

"Not on your life. That thing ain't natural."

"That's blood there."

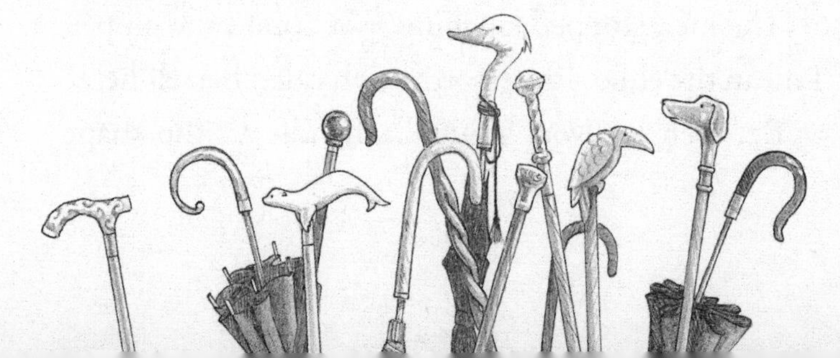

"Look." One of the men pointed to the trail of footprints.

"Little niggle footsteps. It's the nipper."

"She's hid right in there."

They moved toward the umbrella stand. Stella crouched, frozen with fear as they spread out and surrounded her.

"I told you I seen a nipper!" Charlie rubbed his big hands together. "Come on out, little girl. We won't hurt you." The others laughed. He thrust his hand in behind the umbrellas and walking sticks. His big sausage fingers clutched the air just above Stella's head, groped around, and connected with her cheek.

She bit his hand as hard as she could. It tasted of sweat and dirt. He yelled and the hand disappeared.

"Grab one of them there sticks, Charlie. Winkle her out."

There was a rattle, and a walking stick poked in behind the umbrellas and jabbed her ribs. "Out you come, brat." The stick poked her again. She yelped.

"Gentlemen." It was the Professor. Stella couldn't see him, but she could hear his quiet voice. "What is happening?"

The men stopped laughing. "We found the nipper. I mean the child, Professor. She's hidden herself here."

Between an ivory umbrella handle in the shape

of a parrot's head and a leather shooting stick, Stella caught a glimpse of the Professor. He was standing some distance away, in the doorway of the sunroom. He had one hand on the shoulder of the thin, pale boy.

He saw the hand of glory in the puddle.

"Remove that from the water immediately," he ordered, his face stiff and angry. And then he said, more urgently, "Immediately! Is that blood? It is extinguishing the flames. Quickly!"

The masked men hesitated. Two more flames sizzled and died. The Professor cursed, strode quickly across the entrance hall, and reached down for the hand. As his fingers touched it, the last flame hissed, spat, and went out.

He scooped it up. "Get that child. Now." He placed the hand upright on the table and felt in his pockets for matches. He lit one and held the flame to the tip of one of the twisted fingers. The match flickered out. He cursed under his breath and tried again.

The masked men began to pull walking sticks and umbrellas from the stand and throw them onto the floor. But already the air was lighter and clearer and the hotel was stirring. Confused voices came from somewhere nearby. At the desk, Mr. Blenkinsop grunted, coughed, and woke up. He looked around the entrance hall in bewilderment.

"Gentlemen?" He wiped a hand over his face and got to his feet. "What—what is happening?"

The Professor whipped the unlit hand off the table, wrapped it in his handkerchief, and pushed it into an inner pocket of his coat. He said, in a low, angry voice, "You've bungled this, you imbeciles. Get that child. Quickly."

The umbrella stand began to rock. Hands clutched at Stella. She shrank away from them. One of the men pulled her arm.

A maid appeared from the back stairs, her hair disheveled. "Mr. Blenkinsop, Mr. Blenkinsop!"

"What? What?" General Carruthers came stumping down the stairs, waving his stick. "Robbers! Dacoits! Thuggees! After them!"

More residents and servants appeared on the landing.

The Professor said, "Too late. Go!" His face was tight with fury. The masked men recoiled from him, turned, and ran. They all piled out the front door and escaped into the dark. The Professor gripped the thin boy's shoulder to stop him from following them.

The hotel was awake. Heads poked out over the banisters. Residents and servants in dressing gowns and nightcaps were coming down the staircase.

Colonel Fforbes appeared, his magnificent mustache confined in a complicated-looking hairnet.

"Thieves!" shouted the Professor. "A gang of thieves in the hotel!"

"But, sir . . ." Mr. Blenkinsop sounded confused. "You were with them. . . . What were you . . . ?"

One of the maids screamed and fainted dramatically, and the others clustered around. Lady Clottington's nasty little dog, Sir Oswald, shot down the staircase, growling ferociously, and bit Mr. Blenkinsop's ankle. He shrieked. Lady Clottington's maid, her hair in rag curlers, tried to pull the dog off. Sir Oswald let go of Mr. Blenkinsop's ankle and snapped at her hand instead. She squealed. General Carruthers, Colonel Fforbes, and several of the male servants stood in the open doorway, shouting into the darkness outside.

Unseen in the confusion, Stella crawled out from behind the umbrella stand and tiptoed around the bustling crowd, staying close to the wall, keeping as far from the Professor as she could. She hugged the Atlas and Mr. Filbert's package to her chest.

The Professor watched her. Their eyes met for a second. He moved toward her, through the milling people.

With an earsplitting screech, Colonel Fforbes's

macaw, Wellington, flapped into the entrance hall with a flurry of ancient, moth-eaten feathers. Two of the servants ran to catch him as he flew past, and banged their heads together. The fainting maid awoke for a moment, shrieked, and fainted again.

Stella darted between the maids, who were clustered, gasping and giggling, around the manager's desk. She clutched at Mr. Blenkinsop's arm, shook it to get his attention, and when he bent down to her, she whispered urgently, "In the conservatory. Mr. Filbert. He needs help. He's been hurt."

"In the conservatory?" He looked bewildered.

She nodded, and started to say more. But the Professor was approaching, his long fingers reaching toward her, clutching the air.

Mr. Blenkinsop turned to him. "Sir?" he said.

The Professor hesitated.

Breathless, Stella turned away, ducked between the maids again, and scrambled up the stairs as fast as she could. Residents and servants dashed here and there. Stella glimpsed Lady Ogilvy and her maid peering out of a room on the second floor. Lady Ogilvy was hardly recognizable in her lace nightcap, and without her wig and teeth.

Stella ran, panting, all the way up to the third floor.

Nobody had followed her.

It was much quieter here at the top of the hotel. The commotion downstairs was just an echo of distant voices. The passageway was deserted. Stella hurried along to the Aunts' parlor door. She pressed her ear against it and then opened it, slipped through, and locked the door behind her.

The Aunts were still sleeping. She could hear snoring whines from Aunt Temperance, grunts from Aunt Condolence, and deep thundering from Aunt Deliverance.

She crept across the parlor to Aunt Condolence and Aunt Temperance's room, opened the door, and tiptoed between the sleeping Aunts to her own bedroom. She was very relieved to find the key in the lock. She could not have managed to climb out the window and along the ledge again; she was too shaky and frightened. Silently she opened the door, locked it behind her, and collapsed onto her bed.

For a minute or two she listened. There was nothing to hear but snoring. Nothing disturbed the Aunts' sleep. Nobody had followed her. She was safe.

She got up from her bed and poked the Atlas and Mr. Filbert's package under the mattress, pushing them in as far as she could reach. It wasn't the best hiding place, but it would do for now, until she could return the package to Mr. Filbert. She thought for a second, and then pushed in the door key as well. There would be trouble in the morning when Ada came to unlock the door and found the key gone, but that could not be helped.

She inspected her feet. They were filthy, but the bleeding seemed to have stopped. She crawled in under the cold bedcovers. She still felt shaky. Her legs were aching and her feet hurt, her ribs were bruised, and she was so tired.

She curled up and pulled the eiderdown over her head.

It was a long time before she stopped shivering and fell asleep.

Six

Stella woke from a frightening dream full of horrible, twisting, burning black hands to hear whispering voices outside her bedroom. She turned over and sat up. Pale grayish morning sunshine glanced in through the window. She blinked and rubbed her eyes. Then she climbed out of bed, tiptoed to the door, and pressed her ear against it. It was Ada and some of the hotel servants, in the Aunts' bedroom.

"Dead!"

"No!"

"They found him just lying there. Flat out like a cold kipper!"

"Saints preserve us!"

Stella pressed her hand to her mouth. Dead? Who was dead?

The door handle rattled, making her jump. Ada's voice said, "Where is that dratted key?"

Stella darted back to her bed and reached underneath the mattress for the key. She ran silently over and pushed it under the door. Then she scrambled back into bed, pulled the eiderdown up to her chin, and closed her eyes.

The door handle rattled again. "Get that key from the other door, will you, Polly? They're all the same."

"There it is, Ada," said one of the housemaids. "It's fallen out."

The key turned in the lock, and Ada came into the room. "Morning, miss."

Stella opened her eyes and yawned. She hoped it was convincing. "Good morning, Ada."

She could hear the housemaids still whispering just outside the door.

"Murder! Thieves? Police? I ask you!"

"Ohh, I know!"

"What's happened, Ada?" Stella asked, trying to sound as if she had been sleeping all night and knew nothing at all about anything.

Ada closed the door firmly behind her, marched across to the window, drew the curtains back, and looped the tassels in place. "Nothing to concern yourself with, miss," she said. She opened the wardrobe and rummaged through Stella's clothes.

"But . . ."

"Up you get, miss." Ada laid a chemise, stays, stockings, a petticoat, another petticoat, a dress with gray and blue stripes, and a pinafore over the back of the chair. "Come on. I've no time to waste this morning."

Polly, one of the younger housemaids, came in with the brass can of hot water and filled the jug on the washstand. She jerked her head and said, "She's calling for you, Ada."

Aunt Deliverance's bell jangled. Ada pointed to Stella and said, "Will you get her up and dressed, Polly? Be a love. I'm run off my feet this morning," and to Stella, over her shoulder as she left the room, she said, "A proper wash, miss, not just a lick and a promise, if you know what's good for you."

Stella climbed out of bed.

Polly gave a little shriek. "Miss! Look at your nightgown!"

Stella looked down. There was grime all down the front of her nightgown and blood spots on the hem. Her legs and feet were streaked with dirt.

Polly twitched the nightgown off over Stella's head. She held up the filthy garment. "I've never seen the like. All over with muck. What have you been up to, miss?"

"Nothing, Polly."

Polly giggled. "I should tell Ada about this, miss."

"Please don't, Polly," said Stella, shivering in her vest and drawers. But she knew Polly would not get her into trouble. Polly was kind. She had an open, smiling face, and she would sometimes tell Stella gossip from the servants' hall, and scandalous stories from the magazines she loved to read, and sometimes old fairy tales of drowned villages out in the marsh, and sea monsters, and mermaids.

Polly shook her head and bundled up the nightgown. "You're safe with me, miss. I won't land you in strife. Nobody will notice a nightgown, not with everything going on this morning. I'll sneak it into the laundry." She laid an oilcloth over the carpet and poured water into the bowl. Stella dipped a sponge in the water, bent down, and started to wipe the dirt off her legs and feet.

"What's happening, Polly?" she asked.

"I shouldn't tell you, miss," said Polly, giggling again.

"Oh, go on, Polly."

Polly looked over at the door, and then said in a low voice, "Well, miss. Thieves got into the hotel last night."

"Ohh!" Stella tried to sound surprised.

"And after, they found a gentleman lying dead! And ever so many things smashed to pieces!"

"Dead? Who?"

"It was that foreign gentleman, Mr. Filbert. He was lying in the conservatory. Dead as a doormat. And all them flowerpots busted to bits around him."

Mr. Filbert dead! Stella dropped the sponge and pressed her hand to her mouth.

"Are you all right, miss? You've gone ever so pale."

Stella heard her voice say, "Yes," and she watched her hand reach down and pick up the sponge, but inside she felt hollow. He had been alive. She had spoken to him. And now he was dead.

"It's horrible, isn't it, miss? Right here in the hotel. Everything's arsey-versey this morning. Half the servants' hall are plain hysterical. People are talking about giving notice. We'll all be murdered in our beds, they say." Polly sounded as if she welcomed the idea. "It's just like in that *Varney the Vampyre; or, The Feast of Blood.*"

Stella washed and dried her face and hands and started to get dressed. She felt dazed. Could she have done something to save Mr. Filbert? She pulled on her chemise, stays, and stockings.

"That new gentleman, the tall one? Already gone. Didn't stay the night." Polly helped with the stays and chemise and the petticoats, connecting the buttons and loops and tying the ribbons. She bunched up the dress and dropped it over Stella's head.

The Professor, thought Stella. She was relieved he had gone away. When her head came out from the muffling folds of stiff fabric, she said, "He's gone?"

Polly smoothed out the skirt and started fastening the long row of tiny buttons down the back of the dress. "Something odd about that gentleman, if you ask me. That boy of his looked frightened of his own shadow, poor little chap." She finished buttoning the dress and shook out the pinafore. "The police are coming," she went on. "Perhaps they'll make an arrest. Perhaps they'll arrest Mr. Blenkinsop." She giggled. "They've left poor Mr. Filbert lying right there in the conservatory. Nothing is to be touched. The door's locked, and James is watching it. Ready for the detectives. For clues, miss," Polly said with some relish. She pushed Stella's arms into the pinafore and tied the ribbons. "Clues for the detectives. Like in *The Haunted Churchyard; or, the Mystery of the Manchurian Dwarf.*"

She brushed Stella's hair. "Nice gentleman, that Mr. Filbert. Proper old-fashioned. Strange, though. He paid for his room with golden guineas. And there were more in his luggage. Two hundred years old, Mr. Fortescue says, and covered with earth. Like they'd been dug up. But gold is gold, he says." She tied Stella's hair back with a ribbon and said, "That's you done, miss. It's past breakfast time. Everything's late this morning. I've got to get on."

"Thank you, Polly," said Stella. She sat down to pull on her slippers. It was hard to believe that Mr. Filbert was dead.

Dead.

And she had his little package. *Hide it. Keep it safe,* he had said. But what was she to do with it now?

The breakfast room was buzzing with anxious chatter, hammering noises, and the sounds of broken furniture being dragged around. Stella ate stolidly though her breakfast of plain porridge, bread with a thin scrape of butter, and weak, milky tea (Aunt Deliverance believed rich foods like jam and sugar and eggs were unwholesome for children), and listened to the conversations at the neighboring tables. Many of the residents were twittering like startled birds, saying things like *Goodness gracious me* and *Who would have thought?*

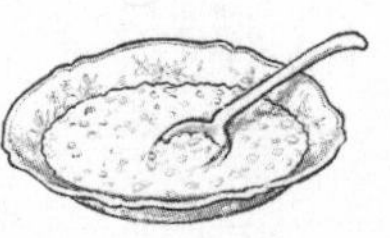

"You were so very heroic, General Carruthers,"

said Lady Ogilvy in a breathy, quavering voice.

"Took to their heels, blasted goose-livered Bashi-Bazouks," said the general, attacking his breakfast bloater with enthusiasm.

"Had the blighters on the run, ha-ha," said Colonel Fforbes. He poked a deviled kidney into his mouth and chewed it up.

"It's all very unsettling," said Aunt Temperance. Her rolling eye swept around in an agitated manner. "That poor foreigner."

Aunt Condolence's Particular Patent Corset twanged as she swallowed a big mouthful of ham and eggs. "Most unsettling," she said.

Stella put down her spoon. Should she say something? Should she tell them about the Professor? She started to say, "I saw—"

"Silence, child," snapped Aunt Deliverance. "There is no necessity for vulgar chitchat." She took an angry bite from a triangle of toast and marmalade and added, "And do not slouch."

After breakfast it began to rain, and so the Aunts could not set out for their daily promenade along the Front. Stella escaped to her bedroom, shut the door, and pulled Mr. Filbert's little package out from under her mattress. The string was knotted tightly. She worked at it with her fingers and then her teeth, and at last she managed to loosen it. Her fingers trembled as she unwrapped the oilcloth and uncovered a smaller package, wrapped in a piece of crinkled, yellowish paper. She glanced toward the door, but she could still hear the Aunts' voices in the parlor, disapproving of the weather. She was safe for the moment. She unfolded the paper quickly.

Inside was a small bottle. It was round and silvery, perhaps two inches across, and slightly iridescent, like a fish scale, or the mother-of-pearl back of her hairbrush. Etched into the surface of the bottle was a curved pattern, like the coils of a serpent.

The little bottle was corked and sealed tightly with red wax. It was heavier than it looked, and as smooth as glass. She held it up to the window. It sparkled in the grayish daylight. She shook it and heard a whispering noise, as if something were slithering over wet sand or shingle. Dark shapes flickered across the wallpaper. A sinuous shape seemed to move inside the bottle, but it was difficult to see. It was dark and silvery at the same time. Perhaps it was only a shadow.

It was beautiful, but it made her skin prickle.

Mr. Filbert had tried to protect it. He had asked her to keep it safe. And she had promised.

And now he was dead.

She folded her fingers over it and held it tightly in the palm of her hand.

Seven

It rained all morning. Raindrops streamed down the window as Stella practiced the pianoforte. Aunt Condolence sat beside her and rapped her smartly on the knuckles every time she played a wrong note, which was often. The piece she was learning, "Waltz for the Pretty Flowers," seemed even harder than usual, and by the end of it, Aunt Condolence was furious and Stella was in tears.

After luncheon (Mock Turtle Soup, Collared Eels, Pickled Tongue and Vegetable Marrows, Cabinet Pudding, and Custard), the rain stopped and the Aunts were able to take their promenade along the Front. Pale sunshine glinted on the little white-capped waves, but the breeze was cold and damp, and dark clouds loomed in the distance. Aunt Deliverance's beady black eyes peered out from a cocoon of shawls and blankets. Ada pushed the bath chair. Aunt Temperance and Aunt Condolence walked beside it and Stella followed behind.

The Aunts always walked down the hill from the Hotel Majestic and then along the Front, past all the smaller hotels, the pleasure gardens, and the pier all the way to the lighthouse. Then they turned and walked back.

Stella liked looking at the sea. It was sometimes gray, sometimes grayish-blue or green, and often there were sailing ships or steamers. The Front was generally busy. There were many convalescents huddled in invalid chairs, old ladies with tiny dogs, and nursemaids pushing perambulators full of muffled-up babies.

Occasionally a young gentleman hurtled along on a high-wheeled bicycle, and the Aunts and all the other old ladies twittered disapprovingly. Sometimes a file of neatly dressed girls from Miss Mallard's Academy for Young Ladies walked past with a grim-looking governess, and that was always interesting. Stella had often thought it would be agreeable to do her lessons with other girls. But from the look of them, the girls from Miss Mallard's Academy had a miserable time. They walked two by two, their gloved hands folded primly and their eyes down, and they never whispered to one another or smiled.

Her favorite part of the promenade was the pier. It stretched out over the sea, the little waves frothing around its elegant, spindly legs. It had curly lampposts that seagulls liked to perch on, and stalls selling cockles and pies and vividly colored sweets. Cheerful, tinny music came from a barrel organ and the steam-powered merry-go-round. At the end of the pier was a theater. It had white domes and fluttering flags. It looked like a palace.

Stella longed to walk out along the pier. But it cost a penny, which she did not have, and Aunt Deliverance said it was Quite Vulgar, so she could only gaze from the Front as they walked past every day. At the entrance to the pier was a gate with turnstiles. The walls on either side were covered with posters and playbills, pasted over one another:

Signor Capelli's
Educated Cats
ASTONISHING
PERFORMANCES!

Monsieur Sabatine
Will balance on his Teeth a real
LIVING DONKEY!

THE ALMONTE BROTHERS
Eccentric and Startling
Acrobatic Tumbling

Beautiful
Abyssinian Lady

Aunt Deliverance said, "Don't dawdle, child," as they walked briskly past and along the Front, past the private villas and boardinghouses and fishing boats, all the way to the shipwreck memorial (ERECTED TO COMMEMORATE THE CALAMITOUS WRECK OF THE CHARLOTTE, 1752, 140 SOULS LOST) below the lighthouse. The shipwreck memorial marked the edge of Withering-by-Sea. Beyond it lay the marsh, which stretched as far as the horizon.

Ada heaved the bath chair around, and they started back.

As they drew level with the pier again, an autocratic voice called "Good afternoon," and an elderly lady hove into sight. It was Miss Ollerenshaw, an acquaintance of Aunt Deliverance, a resident of the Hotel Imperial. Miss Ollerenshaw wore a ruffled black dress, a hat decorated with a huge swaying bunch of curly black feathers, a black fur tippet, and several strings of jet beads. Her maid walked behind her, clutching the leads of three yapping Scottish terriers and carrying a pile of rugs and shawls and an enormous black umbrella.

Stella made a bob and said, "How do you do, Miss Ollerenshaw?" and after a minute or two (as the Aunts and Miss Ollerenshaw talked about the weather, and then about how they had to watch the maids to ensure they did their work properly, and then about the scandalous events at the Hotel Majestic), she drifted away and gazed at the posters:

Extraordinary Feats!
Miss Addie Scarsey
Charming Velocipedist

WONDROUS CURIOSITIES!
AN IMMENSELY LARGE
Royal Bengal Tiger

There was a picture of the tiger. It had staring eyes and impressive teeth and claws. Stella was admiring it when another poster caught her attention. With a jolt, she recognized the thin face staring out of the picture. It was the Professor. He was dressed in black. He was standing beside a pillar, which held a rabbit and a bowl of goldfish, and on his other side was a draped curtain. He had one hand raised and seemed to have lightning shooting out of it. Stella read:

Professor Starke
Conjuring and Wonderful Delusions

Marvels of Magic!

The Magnificent Cabinet of MYSTERIES

The CHINESE Snuffbox

The Enchanted Handkerchiefs

BEHEADING A LADY

The World of Spirits REVEALED!

Stella stared blankly at the poster. The Professor was a magician. It made him seem even more frightening and mysterious.

She thought of Mr. Filbert's silver bottle, hidden

safely under her mattress at the hotel. What could it be that it was so important to the Professor? Perhaps he would do magic to try to discover where it was. Perhaps he was doing magic right now.

As she pondered this disconcerting thought, she heard a whimper. It sounded like a seagull or a cat. She looked around. There was nothing close-by. She heard the sound again. It was a kind of sob, and it seemed to come from under her feet. She walked to the railing, leaned over, and looked down at the beach.

A small figure crouched in the shadow under the pier. His arms were wrapped around his knees, and his head was down.

Stella looked over her shoulder. The Aunts were still deep in conversation with Miss Ollerenshaw. Aunt Condolence was pointing toward her stomach and making a twisting gesture with her fingers. They had started on the topic of their health, which would certainly keep them occupied for some time.

Stella hung over the railing and called, "Are you all right?"

He looked up. She recognized him. He was the thin, pale boy who had been with the Professor at the hotel. His face seemed very white against the dark shadow under the pier, and there were black smudges beneath his eyes. He shrugged miserably and looked down again.

Stella asked, "How did you get down there?"

He didn't answer, but she spied a rusty ladder bolted to the seawall. She looked back at the Aunts and Miss Ollerenshaw. Aunt Condolence was making a vigorous gesture with her hands as if she were wringing out a dishcloth, and the others were nodding. They were clearly still discussing Aunt Condolence's insides.

Stella pulled off her gloves. "I'm coming down," she said, and climbed over the railing.

Eight

Stella climbed down the rusty ladder. Her feet crunched on the shingly beach. The tide was in, and there was only a narrow strip of sand. The waves made a rhythmic hissing, tinkling noise, turning over the pebbles and frothing around the legs of the pier.

She scrunched over to where the boy was sitting. He was hugging his knees, looking out to sea. He wore a thick coat and a grimy woolen scarf.

"I'm Stella. Are you all right?"

"Ben." He shrugged.

"I saw you last night. In the hotel."

"I know."

She sat down beside him on the pebbles. It was cold in the shadow under the pier. She hugged her coat around herself and said, "You were looking into the ink." She cupped her hands together.

"Scrying." He sniffed miserably.

She waited for him to say more, and when he did not, she asked, "What's scrying?"

"I can see things in the ink."

"What kind of things?"

"Things that have happened. Whatever he tells me. He makes me do it." He rubbed his hands over his face. His fingers were still stained black. After a moment he said, "I saw that gentleman hide the little thing in that pot."

"And now he's dead," said Stella.

Ben nodded. "I know. I saw. It was horrible." His voice faltered. "I couldn't help it." He put his head down, his shoulders shaking.

She reached over and patted his arm. "It wasn't your fault."

He did not lift his head.

She patted him again. They sat together in silence for several minutes. Stella wasn't sure what to say.

There was a squeak, and a tiny black kitten poked its face out of the folds of Ben's scarf. Stella touched the kitten's head with one finger.

Ben lifted his tearstained face. "Shadow," he said, and gently unhooked the kitten's claws from the entangling scarf. "She was sleeping. She's my cat."

"Shadow." Stella stroked the little kitten. She was

quite black, with sea-green eyes. She arched her back and rubbed her chin against Stella's hand, then bit her finger, quite hard.

"Ouch!" said Stella.

"Found her in the street, all by herself. My gran had a black cat just like her. She's clever. I'm going to train her to do tricks," said Ben. "She likes you. She can tell you're fey."

"Does she?" asked Stella doubtfully, sucking her finger. Then she said, "I beg your pardon?"

"She can tell you're fey." He looked at her. His eyes were a peculiar pale gray. "You know. Fey. Uncanny. Cats can tell." The kitten scrambled up onto his shoulder, purring. He stroked her, and she made some high-pitched squeaking noises and bit him on the ear. He went on, "Fey. Like me." And when Stella shrugged, he said, "You must be. I knew straightaway. Because the hand o' glory didn't make you sleep. It don't work if you're fey."

Stella shrugged again. "I don't know what you mean. What's fey?"

Ben wiped his nose with the back of his hand. He said, "You know. My gran said fey is like an echo of the old magic. Not powerful anymore. Not like back when there was fairies and giants and sorcerers and that. Just a tiny trickly bit. Some people say 'touched.'

Second sight. You can see things that ain't there."

"I can't do anything like that," said Stella.

Ben said, "P'raps it's something else with you. It goes in your family."

Stella shook her head. "No," she said.

"For me, my gran was part selkie. I get it from her."

"What's selkie?"

"They were seal people. They could change into seals, in the sea. From Scotland. They could see the future in still water, Gran said."

Stella felt the back of her neck prickling. She suddenly remembered Aunt Condolence saying, *Disgraceful, even for a half—* And she had stopped. But what had she been about to say? A half what?

Stella said firmly, "But there's no such thing as seal people. And nobody can see into the future."

"Not anymore," said Ben. "Of course not. But in the old days. Long ago." He tickled Shadow's chin. "Like with me, I'm not a selkie, but I'm fey. I can't turn into a seal, I can't see the future, but I can sometimes see things that happened, in the ink. My gran and me, we had an act. She did scrying with a glass ball. She learned me. We told fortunes." Ben gave a sudden grin. "It was a good act." He said, in a whispery, foreign voice, "*Seven crows will fly over your roof. A toad will cross your path. A dark stranger will surprise you*. It was good. But then she died, and I went in the orphanage." He rubbed his nose. "It was terrible there. And then the Professor came and he took me away. He knew our act, he remembered me. He needs me for scrying. He wants that little bottle."

"Why does he want it? Do you know what's in it?"

Ben said, "Don't open it."

"I won't—"

"No." He looked at her seriously. "Don't open it. It's bad. He found out about it in an old book. In Latin. The bottle was buried under this big old tree, out on the marsh. Where that village got drowned. You know?"

Stella nodded. She had heard from Polly the frightening story of the village that had drowned in the marsh. And how the church bells still rang on stormy nights, even though the church had been empty for years and the bells were gone.

Ben went on, "We went out there at night. Cut down the tree and dug up the roots to find it. But that old cove took it."

"Mr. Filbert?"

"I don't think that's his real name. Dryad, the Professor called him. He came out of nowhere when we was digging up the roots of the tree, and he grabbed the bottle and he scarpered. The Professor lost him, but then he found out he was in that hotel, and so we went there. But the cove wouldn't say where he hid it. So the men looked for it while the hand o' glory was lit and everyone was sleeping. Then the Professor made me scry. He was in a right fury when he didn't find it in that pot. He's got a sword in that stick, and he just pulled it out and stabbed the cove right in the chest." Ben rubbed his hands over his face again, leaving black marks. "It was horrible."

"I've got—"

"Don't tell me." He clutched her arm. "Don't tell me you've got it or where it is. Don't tell me nothing. If I know, I'll tell him. He'll make me tell him."

"It's just—"

"No." He let go of her arm. "Don't tell me. He'll make me scry anyway, and then I'll see where it is, and I'll tell him. You can't trust me at all." He looked out to sea. His expression was bleak.

Stella stroked Shadow's head. Poor Ben. The Professor sounded worse than a hundred Aunts. After a minute, she said, "Can't you run away from him?"

He shook his head miserably. "He'd come after me." Then he added, in a broken voice, "I ain't brave enough."

"The police are coming today. Perhaps they'll arrest him."

"He ain't worried about them."

She said, "I saw the poster. He's a magician."

Ben nodded. "On the stage."

"Can he really do magic?" asked Stella.

Ben shook his head again. "It's just tricks," he said. "Mirrors and clockwork. He builds things. He's clever."

"What about the hand of glory?" asked Stella. "That wasn't a trick."

"No," said Ben with a shudder. "He collects things too. Bad things. That's made out of the hand of a hanged man. It makes people sleep. And you can only put out the flames with milk or blood."

Stella remembered the blood in the puddle, and the sputtering flames. She nodded. "Is he fey, the Professor? It didn't make him go to sleep."

"That's because it was him what lit it. He ain't fey. It's just tricks he builds, and old things he collects."

"Where are you staying?" she asked.

He pointed a thumb over his shoulder. "Boarding-house back there. Flanagan's, it's called. Do you live in that hotel?"

She nodded. "With my Aunts. They drink the water and have baths. For their health."

"Drink the water?"

"It's special water. It's revolting. It comes up out of the ground underneath the hotel. It's famous. People drink it for their health." Stella giggled. "Before this, in another hotel, they ate only white things, like turnips and milk puddings and tapioca, and they had to drink potato juice for breakfast. And before that, we were up in the mountains. They had cold-air baths, and there was an Influence Machine, and they had to sleep with their windows open. Sometimes the snow came in."

"And that makes them better?"

"Not so far," said Stella. She raked her fingers through the smooth beach pebbles, and after a moment, she asked, "Do you know what it is? Do you know what's in the bottle?"

He nodded reluctantly. "Professor's always on about it. He talks about giants and fairies and sea serpents. And sorcerers from the old days. They were full of magic. They could turn into birds or fishes. And there was one sorcerer, he could turn into a sea serpent. Professor's always on about him, says he could make the weather, storms and that. The Grimpen Sorcerer, he was called, and—"

Before he could say more, an angry voice came from above. "Miss. Miss. Where are you, drat you?"

"It's Ada!" she gasped, jumping to her feet. 'She can't see you. I'm not allowed to talk to anyone ever—"

Ben gave her another grin. "I'll get out of the way." He scooped up Shadow, scrambled up the shingle to the seawall, and ducked behind one of the pier's iron legs. "Go on," he said.

"Good-bye, Ben. Good-bye, Shadow."

"Bye, Stella."

She waved a hand at him and scrunched out from under the shelter of the pier into a steady drizzle. She hadn't noticed it had started raining again. The Aunts would be furious and wet.

"Ada!" she called. "I'm down here."

She started to climb up the rusty ladder. "I'm here, Ada."

An angry, dripping face appeared over the top of the railing. "What on earth are you doing down there, miss?"

"Nothing, Ada."

"Always making work for people. Sniggling off like that. Always hiding. It's pouring rain, and there you are, creeping around like I don't know what. Why can't you behave?" Ada grasped Stella's arm and hauled her over the railing.

"I'm sorry, Ada."

"I've been up and down calling you for twenty minutes. I'm wet through. Your Aunts have gone back to the hotel. Didn't you hear me?" said Ada. She took hold of Stella's shoulders and shook her until her teeth rattled, then gripped her arm and strode back along the deserted Front, pulling Stella with her. The sea had disappeared into a gray, misty haze, and the rain was becoming heavier.

Stella said, "I'm sorry, Ada," again, but Ada did not answer.

They climbed the hill to the hotel, splashing through puddles. Water dripped off the brim of Stella's hat and trickled down her neck. Her hair was plastered down her back. Ada was even wetter, and her grip on Stella's arm was tight and angry. She marched along the drive and in through the front door of the hotel. She snatched off Stella's dripping coat and hat, pulled off her own things, shook them out, and hung them up.

She grasped Stella's arm again and dragged her across the entrance hall toward the bathhouse.

"Where are we going?" asked Stella. Her wet shoes skidded on the marble floor.

"Your Aunts want to see you. They'll be in the wave bath."

Stella's heart sank, and she shivered. Tendrils of mist swirled around her, and the wave bath machine clanked ominously in the distance.

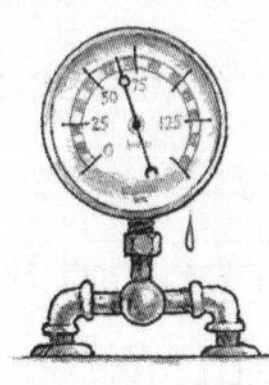

Nine

Ada marched Stella along the tiled corridor. Hot, misty air drifted out of doorways, icy winds whirled around unexpectedly, and water dripped.

Stella said, "Are they very angry, Ada?"

"What do you think, miss?" snapped Ada discouragingly.

She pulled Stella through an archway and down a short flight of slippery stairs. The wave bath machine made a slow, grunting *clank, clank, clank*. A deep-sounding noise that Stella could hear through her feet and in her teeth. Thick steam billowed around. Drops of warm water condensed on the blue-and-gold mosaic dolphins that decorated the arched ceiling. They trickled down the tiled walls and pooled on the floor.

Stella blinked and coughed.

"I found the child, ma'am, Miss Temperance, Miss Condolence." Ada spoke loudly above the noise. She made a bob and gave Stella a push toward the row of baths.

Stella took a few nervous steps and stopped.

Clank, clank. Each time the machine made another slow cycle, the six baths rocked forward and back. In each bath, waves formed and broke over the foot and then over the head. Water splashed out of the baths and trickled down the drain, and more water poured in from above.

Three baths were empty. Three baths were full of Aunts. They were wrapped and strapped up like enormous puddings, basting in the steaming water.

Clank, clank. The machine lifted the row of baths. The Aunts' heads were raised up, and a wave broke over their legs and feet. They all glared at Stella.

"Come closer," commanded Aunt Deliverance. "Ada. Where did you find her?"

"Under the pier, ma'am."

Aunt Deliverance studied Stella, her eyes like two little currants. For some reason, Aunt Deliverance seemed even more frightening strapped helplessly into the wave bath like this than she did wheeling around in her bath chair. Only her pasty, boiled-looking face showed, and only when the bath rocked forward. The rest of her was streaming wet canvas, straps, and buckles.

"Stand up straight, child. Don't hunch your shoulders," she snapped. She looked unusually grim. Aunt Temperance and Aunt Condolence made outraged sniffing noises.

Stella straightened up, put her hands behind her back and her ankles together.

"You are repeatedly disobedient, willful, obstinate . . ." *Clank, clank,* the bath slowly rocked backward and the Aunts' faces disappeared from sight. There was a surge and a splash. *Clank, clank.* ". . . intractable and ungrateful," Aunt Deliverance went on as she rose up again, streaming with water. "Look at the state of your clothes. You seem to have no idea how a lady should behave. Your lessons show no improvement at all, and Condolence tells me your performance on the pianoforte is getting worse . . ."

"Yes, indeed," said Aunt Condolence.

Another wave broke over their feet, and the bath clanked and rocked backward. A wave crashed again. *Clank, clank.* Aunt Deliverance continued, ". . . which hardly seems possible. Temperance tells me you constantly question her during lesson time. Sordid curiosity! Yesterday you missed luncheon, and today Ada finds you skulking under the pier. Disgraceful! And dangerous."

Aunt Deliverance glared at Stella as the bath tipped backward.

Stella stared back miserably. *Clank, clank.*

"I will *not* have any more of this behavior." Aunt Deliverance appeared again, looking thunderous. "You will be dutiful, punctual, and obedient. You will apply yourself to your lessons, and I will see improvement in your conduct. No tea today, bread and water for your supper. And you will spend two hours every morning practicing your deportment to correct that slouch."

Stella said, "Yes, Aunt Deliverance," and looked sadly down at her waterlogged shoes.

Friday was Stella's bath night, which was fortunate because she was drenched to the skin and felt shivery and miserable.

The Aunts had a magnificent private bathroom. Tiles with pictures of brilliantly colored birds on them were set in the paneled walls. The taps and pipes were gleaming copper and brass, the gaslights hung with sparkling crystals, and the enormous bath was surrounded with mahogany paneling.

Ada leaned over the bath to fiddle with the levers and taps. The Hotel Majestic was extremely modern, and as well as the Vertical Omnibus and flush-down water closets, it had piped hot water, which meant the servants did not have to carry the water to fill the baths. When the levers were adjusted correctly and the taps were turned, the hot water came sputtering and steaming from a spout in the shape of a dolphin, straight into the bathtub.

The dolphin hissed and shot out a cloud of steam. Ada jumped, muttered something under her breath, and adjusted a lever. The dolphin clanked and gurgled and spluttered and spat. Ada banged it with the side of her hand, and it made a final coughing noise and water gushed into the bath.

As the bath filled, Ada helped Stella undress, not very gently, and tied her hair up. She leaned over to turn off the taps. Stella climbed into the bath and Ada bustled about, muttering under her breath. She took the bundle of wet clothes away and came back with underclothes and a nightgown, and hung them over the back of the chair. "Wash yourself properly. Don't get that hair any wetter, mind, miss," she said, and went away again.

Stella lay back in the warm water. She had not cried when the Aunts had been scolding her, but now, when nobody could see, she let two tears trickle down her face and drip into the bathwater.

It was a familiar, dismal feeling to be in disgrace again. And this time, Aunt Deliverance had been especially furious. Stella sighed, lifted the sponge, and let the water trickle onto her face and wash away the tears.

She wondered what Ben was doing right now. Perhaps he was helping the Professor get ready for the magic show in the theater. Or perhaps the Professor was making him see things in the ink again. Trying to find Mr. Filbert's bottle. Poor Ben. It sounded as if he had a wretched life. The Professor was even more frightening than the Aunts, and more dangerous.

She thought about what Ben had said, that she might be fey. It seemed very unlikely. She couldn't see things that were not there, as he did in the ink. She certainly couldn't do anything like that.

It goes in your family, he had said. His gran was part selkie. There was nothing in the Atlas about selkies, she was sure of that. And nothing in *French Conversation for Young Ladies* either.

Perhaps Polly knew about them.

And were there selkies in her own family? Or something else?

All Stella knew about her parents was that they had died when she was little. The hotel residents sometimes hissed and whispered behind their hands, and Stella had overheard enough scraps of servants' gossip to know there was some kind of secret. Perhaps a scandal. But the Aunts would never answer her questions. *Curiosity is vulgar, silence is golden,* Aunt Deliverance said. Sometimes two or three times a day.

There was a framed daguerreotype in Aunt Deliverance's bedroom, an ancient picture of all three Aunts as very young ladies (but quite recognizable, from their stern and disapproving expressions). On Aunt Condolence's lap sat the fourth sister, a baby with round startled eyes, dressed in an extraordinary quantity of frills and ribbons.

That baby was Stella's mother, Patience.

Stella squeezed the sponge over her face again and thought about the baby in the picture. How could she find out more about her mother? And what about her father? She did not even know his name. Her surname, Montgomery, came from her mother. The Aunts never spoke of her father, but it was clear they disapproved strongly. She had always known he had been somehow disreputable. Or perhaps he had done something disgraceful. But now she wondered, what if it was something else? How could she find out?

Outside the bathroom door the maids were gossiping again. Stella could hear gasps and giggling. There was a knock at the door.

She wiped her face and called, "Come in."

Polly pushed the door open. "Here you are, miss," she said, and put a pile of folded towels on the chair.

"Thank you, Polly." Stella sat up in the bath. "What's happening?"

Polly giggled and said, "I shouldn't tell you, miss. I shouldn't, really."

"Oh, go on, Polly."

Polly perched on the side of the bath. "Well, miss. The police detectives from London are here."

"Ohh," said Stella.

"They're down in the entrance hall right now, talking to Mr. Blenkinsop, and James and Mr. Fortescue."

Stella nodded. Mr. Fortescue was the owner of the hotel.

"Well. When they went to look at poor Mr. Filbert, in the conservatory, you won't believe what they found, miss."

"What?"

Polly lowered her voice to a whisper. "Just old sticks, twisted up, like a scarecrow. In Mr. Filbert's clothes. But no body. And the conservatory locked, miss. And James watching the door."

Stella put her hand to her mouth.

"They've dragged it into the entrance hall. It's lying there now. The police say if there's no body, there's no murder. They think it's a trick. A swizzle. They're going back to London tomorrow."

"But what about Mr. Filbert?" asked Stella, half to herself.

Polly got up from the bath. "Well, miss. It's like in *The Gypsy's Warning; or, Love and Ruin.*" She held up a finger. "Foreigners, miss. You can't tell what they'll get up to. That's what people are saying." She gave another giggle and whisked out of the bathroom.

Stella stared blankly at the empty room. But Mr. Filbert was dead. Ben had seen it happen. He'd seen the Professor stab him in the chest.

After a moment she climbed out of the bath, dried herself roughly, and pulled on her nightclothes. She opened the bathroom door. The Aunts were getting dressed for dinner in their bedrooms. She could hear Aunt Deliverance scolding Ada, and Aunt Condolence's Particular Patent Corset twanging busily.

Stella tiptoed across the empty parlor, pulled open the door, and peeped out. The passage was deserted. She crept along to the main staircase, toward the echoing sound of voices, and leaned over the banister. Below, the entrance hall was crowded with clustered groups of residents and servants.

A body lay in the middle of the patterned marble floor. It was the figure of a man, made from twisted sticks. It was dressed in shirt, trousers, and slippers. The arms were outflung, the back was arched, and in the center of the white shirtfront was a dark, spreading stain.

The face of the figure seemed to be staring straight up at Stella. And although it was formed only from twigs, it was somehow twisted into an expression of horror. Stella felt shaken. She swallowed and tore her gaze away from the grotesque scarecrow. She studied the other people milling around it. From above, Stella could see only the tops of their heads, but she spied two policemen's helmets, and she recognized the gray hair of the housekeeper, Mrs. Abercrombie, fussing around the maids' lace caps, chivvying them back to work.

At the front desk stood Mr. Fortescue, an enormous gentleman with very impressive orange wavy hair. With him were the shiny bald head of Mr. Blenkinsop and the dark, smooth hair of James, the conductor of the Vertical Omnibus. Several men in hats appeared to be asking them angry questions and writing the answers in their notebooks. *The police detectives,* thought Stella.

She started down the staircase. She should tell the police detectives what she had seen and what she knew about the Professor and Mr. Filbert. Would they listen to her?

Quick footsteps from behind made her jump. It was Ada, and she looked furious. She grabbed Stella's arm with a hard hand and dragged her back up the stairs and along to the Aunts' rooms, scolding in an angry undertone.

"What are you up to now, miss?"

"But, Ada—"

"Priggling around in your nightie. Making trouble again."

"I'm sorry, Ada, I was—"

"Hold your tongue, miss."

Ada pulled her along to her bedroom. She picked up the hairbrush and yanked it through Stella's damp, tangled hair, hard enough to make her cry out. When she'd finished, she gave Stella a sharp rap on her head with the brush. "You stay put, miss, or you'll catch it," she snapped. She stalked out of the room, slammed the door, and turned the key in the lock.

Ten

That night Stella tossed and turned, and at last fell into an uneasy sleep. She dreamed of dark water, rippling as if something enormous swam just below the surface. The water swirled and tugged and tried to pull her under. She could not breathe. She woke in a panic, shaking and gasping for air.

Heart thumping, she untangled herself from the sheets. The eiderdown had fallen onto the floor. She got up and went to the window. At night Ada always drew the curtains firmly closed, but whenever Stella was sent to bed early in disgrace (which was often), she pulled them open again so she could lie in bed and look out at the sky.

She heaved the window open and breathed the outside air. The rain had stopped, but the night was misty and there were no stars. She felt shaky and unsettled.

Down on the terrace, a dark shape moved into the shadow behind one of the stone lions. Stella stiffened. *Probably a fox,* she told herself. *No need to be so jumpy.* She watched for several moments, hardly blinking, but everything was still.

It was freezing. She turned away from the window and knelt down to pull the Atlas and Mr. Filbert's package out from under the mattress. She heaved the eiderdown back onto the bed, crawled underneath, and pulled it up to her chin.

Striking a match, she lit the candle, then unfolded the oilcloth and the paper from Mr. Filbert's package. The little silver bottle sparkled in the candlelight. It was quite beautiful, but it gave her a very uneasy feeling.

Dark shapes flickered across the wallpaper, like shoals of tiny fish. What could be inside? And why did the Professor want it so desperately? Ben had started to tell her about the Grimpen Sorcerer when Ada had called her away. She wished she could talk to him again.

She touched the wax seal. *Don't open it,* Ben had said. But somehow she knew already that whatever was inside the little bottle must never get out.

And that she must find a safer place to hide it.

After a moment, she laid the bottle beside the

candle and picked up the Atlas. She rested it on her knees and opened it at random, at a map dotted with islands. She spelled out the words that stretched across the map, *Frozen Ocean,* and traced the Arctic Circle with her finger. She studied a picture of a walrus on an iceberg. Its superior expression and whiskery face reminded her forcefully of Aunt Deliverance. *The walrus makes the air resound with its bellowing, which is very like that of the bull.* She giggled. That sounded familiar. She traced a passage around King Oscar Land, imagining paddling a canoe through the icy ocean, past whales and seals and herds of bellowing walruses. It was a cheerful image. The Atlas was always comforting.

The Aunts snored rhythmically, and the clock in the parlor struck two.

Stella heard a faint clattering noise from the terrace outside. She climbed out of bed again, tiptoed over to the window, and leaned out.

She thought she saw something move, but she couldn't be sure, and although she watched for a long time, nothing else stirred.

At last, frozen right through, she crept back to bed. She blew out the candle and lay there shivering, curled up tight, clutching Mr. Filbert's bottle and the Atlas, and eventually she fell asleep.

The following morning after breakfast, Stella had two hours of extremely tedious deportment practice.

Aunt Temperance clapped her hands and said, "Head up. Eyes down. Shoulders back," as Stella walked slowly around and around the parlor with *French Conversation for Young Ladies* balanced on top of her head. "Small steps. Small steps. Now stop. Curtsy."

Stella stopped and made a bob, and the book slid off and hit the floor with a bang. She bent, picked it up, and replaced it on her head.

"When I was a girl, we did this with a wineglass of milk on our heads," said Aunt Temperance. "And we never spilled a drop."

Stella nodded. The book fell off.

"You're not concentrating, child."

It was true. Stella wasn't concentrating on balancing the book. She had too many other things to think about. Absentmindedly, she picked it up and put it back on her head. There was so much she didn't know. She wished she could talk to Ben again.

She thought about Mr. Filbert. The Professor had stabbed him, and he had been lying dead on the floor of the conservatory. But the police detectives had found only a scarecrow made of twisted sticks. What did that mean? Had someone replaced Mr. Filbert's dead body with the scarecrow for some reason? Or— Stella stopped in her tracks as she had another thought.

Bang. The book slid off the front of her head and hit the floor again. Aunt Temperance made annoyed clicking noises with her tongue. "Back straight. Head up. Small steps. Concentrate, child."

Stella bent and picked up the book.

Could the Professor have somehow changed Mr. Filbert into sticks? Using magic? It seemed very unlikely. Or perhaps, if Ben could be related to seals (which also seemed very unlikely), then Mr. Filbert might be related to—what? Wicker baskets? Bird nests?

"Aunt Temperance?"

"What is it?"

"Can—I mean, can a person be turned into sticks? Into a scarecrow?"

Aunt Temperance gave a gasp. "Quiet, child."

"Have you heard of the Grimpen—"

"Be quiet!"

"But—"

"Quiet! Don't ask such outrageous questions." Aunt Temperance's rolling eye circled wildly. "We never speak of such things. Never. Curiosity is a sign of a vulgar mind. Pay attention to your deportment." She clapped her hands. "Head up, shoulders back, small steps."

Stella sighed and balanced *French Conversation for Young Ladies* on top of her head again.

"Back straight, eyes down," instructed Aunt Temperance. "Fifty times around the room." She stalked to the door. "When I return from the bathhouse, I expect to see some improvement."

She left the parlor, and Stella immediately stopped walking and stood, staring into space, thinking. Meeting with Ben again would be difficult to arrange. She would have to leave that to chance. But she could find out more about Mr. Filbert. Who was he? Where had he come from?

After a moment, she took the book from her head, went along to her room, and extracted the key from the door. She had overheard Ada say that the bedroom keys were all the same. She compared her key to the one from the Aunts' room. They were identical.

She checked the bathroom, the parlor, Aunt Deliverance's bedroom, and the dressing room where Ada slept. The keys were all the same. Which would be least likely to be missed? She thought for a second, and then went and tucked Ada's key under her mattress.

Now she would be able to escape easily from her room, without having to make the frightening climb out of the window and along the ledge. Tonight she would see if she could find out more about Mr. Filbert. She knew where his room was on the second floor of the hotel. She would go and look through his things. Perhaps she would find a clue to his identity. Perhaps she would discover what his little bottle contained, and what she should do with it. Smiling to herself, she put *French Conversation for Young Ladies* back on top of her head and started circling the parlor again.

It rained steadily all morning. Gray clouds sat sluggishly on the roof of the hotel, and water splashed and dripped from the gutters. Stella sat at the parlor table, sewing and listening to the raindrops hitting the window. She had been sewing the sampler for nearly two years. She had sewn two alphabets in tiny stitches, and a row of numbers, and a depressing verse:

Let me Improve the Hours I have,
Before the Day of Grace is Fled,
There's no Repentance in the Grave
Nor Pardons Offered to the Dead.

It was difficult to read because Aunt Condolence had made Stella unpick it and sew it repeatedly, and the linen was grimy and wrinkled.

Around the alphabets and the verse, and right around the edges of the sampler, Stella had sewn a border of dozens of tiny flowers: violets (which meant modesty), sweetbriar (which meant simplicity), and daisies (which meant patience). Stella would have liked to include some interesting jungle flowers as well, but there were no jungle flowers in Aunt Condolence's little book *The Language of Flowers,* and so they might have meant anything. Most probably something vulgar, Aunt Condolence said. Sewing the flowers had taken months and months.

Now Stella was slowly filling in the spaces between the flowers with little pictures. She had sewn a picture of a soldier in India being eaten up by an angry-looking tiger and an exciting scene of a sailing ship being attacked by a sea monster. Aunt Condolence had not approved of either of these, and so the next picture was a dull man riding a dull horse along a dull road. The man's coat was made of tiny stitches of red silk. The thread kept knotting itself and tangling around the needle. Stella sighed and jabbed the needle through the linen again. It went into her finger and she squeaked.

"Quiet, child," said Aunt Condolence from the other side of the parlor, without looking up.

Stella sucked her finger quietly and eyed Aunt Condolence. She was writing a letter. Her Particular Patent Corset creaked as she reached over and dipped her pen into the ink.

Stealthily, Stella pushed the sampler to one side and took a small piece of linen from her sewing box. She folded it in half and started sewing small, close-together stitches around the sides to make a little pocket.

When she had finished, she sewed on a loop and a button, so it would close properly. It would be just big enough to hold Mr. Filbert's package. She sewed both ends of a length of hair ribbon to the pocket. This way she could wear it around her neck, hidden under her clothes. It was the safest hiding place she could think of.

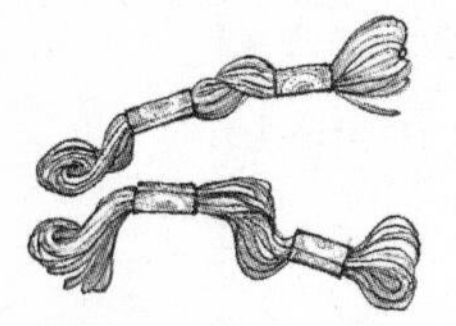

She attached the ribbon as firmly as

she could. When it was quite finished, she poked the pocket into the leg of her drawers and picked up the sampler again. Aunt Condolence had not looked up from her letter. Stella smiled to herself as she stabbed the needle into the linen and made another red silk stitch into the dull horseman's coat.

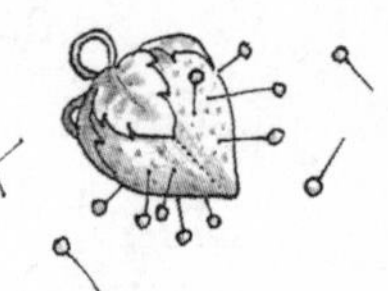

After luncheon (Prince of Wales Soup, Boiled Turbot and Stewed Cabbage, Haricot Mutton, Military Pudding with Sago Sauce), Aunt Deliverance announced that the rain was holding off, and so they set out for their promenade along the Front.

A cold, damp wind was blowing, and Ada tucked extra blankets and shawls around Aunt Deliverance until she looked like an enormous roly-poly pudding. Stella walked behind Ada and the Aunts, Mr. Filbert's package safe in its little pocket around her neck, hidden under her clothes.

As they left the hotel drive and turned into the street, a furtive-looking man leaning against a lamppost whistled loudly. He had pale whiskers, a tall hat, and a heliotrope waistcoat with a pattern of tulips. For a moment his gaze met Stella's, and then he turned his back and walked quickly away.

Stella blinked. Something about the man was familiar. But she couldn't think where she had seen him before.

They headed down the hill and out along the Front. The few people they passed had their heads down and walked briskly. Stella had to skip every few steps to keep up with Ada and the Aunts.

Seagulls rode the wind, swooping and crying. The flags on the pier fluttered; dead leaves and sweets wrappers swirled around.

All along the Front, Stella looked for Ben, but there was no sign of him, nor of the Professor. The pier was almost deserted. White-capped waves crashed onto the shingle. Beyond the pier, fishermen were pulling their boats farther up the beach.

They reached the shipwreck memorial. Ada stopped in the shelter of the lighthouse and tucked in Aunt Deliverance's blankets and shawls. Then she hauled the bath chair around and they headed back into the strengthening icy wind. Dark gray clouds were building up out to sea. A jagged flash of lightning and a crack of thunder made Stella jump. She hugged her arms around herself as she trotted along behind Ada and the Aunts, splashing through puddles.

They reached the hotel just as the rain started. Mr.

Blenkinsop and one of the footmen rushed out into the downpour to help Ada heave Aunt Deliverance and the bath chair up the stairs to the front door.

They rode up to their floor on the Vertical Omnibus. As usual, the lurching ascent made Aunt Deliverance set her mouth in a thin line, Aunt Temperance shut her eyes tightly, and Aunt Condolence clutch her middle and make tiny moaning noises. Stella always enjoyed the ride. It was far more agreeable than climbing the stairs. She liked the clanking, grinding noise and the feeling the ascent gave her, as if her insides were being left behind down below while the rest of her rose up into the air.

"Third floor, ma'am, if you please." James pulled the brake lever. Steam hissed and the Vertical Omnibus jerked to a stop. He opened the paneled door and the curly metal gate, helping Ada maneuver the bath chair out and along the passageway to the Aunts' rooms.

The Aunts' door was ajar. Ada muttered something under her breath. She reached out and pushed the door open. The lock hung, splintered and broken.

Ada took two steps into the Aunts' parlor, stopped dead, and clutched at her throat. "Lawks a bleedin' mercy!" she shrieked. "Thieves!"

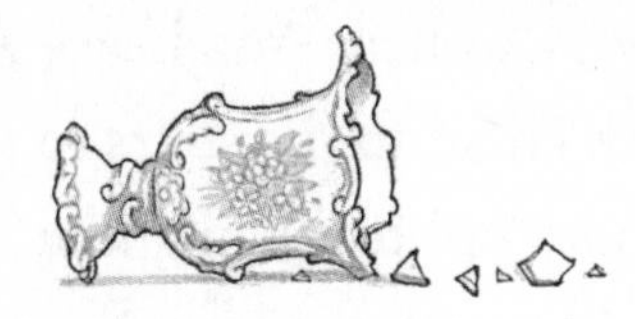

Eleven

Stella followed Ada and the Aunts into the parlor. The room was in disarray. Furniture was overturned, ornaments were scattered, broken china and torn pianoforte music and trampled flowers were littered everywhere.

"Help! Thieves!" Ada rushed out to the hallway, shrieking.

Aunt Temperance made a series of high-pitched squeaks and Aunt Condolence clutched her chest, panting. She leaned against an upended chair. It toppled over and she tumbled to the floor.

"Ada!" bellowed Aunt Deliverance. "Ada!"

Stella picked her way carefully across the parlor to the Aunts' bedroom. Aunt Temperance's bed was pulled out from the wall, the wardrobe was open, and clothes lay strewn in untidy heaps. Jewelry, brushes, and ornaments were scattered across the floor.

Aunt Temperance's glinting lizard brooch caught Stella's eye. Beside it lay a photograph album, green velvet with brass corners. A few photographs had fallen out. Curious, Stella crouched down. The first picture she picked up was of an enormous house, bristling with turrets and chimneys, dark against a looming cloudy sky. In front of the house, a young Aunt Deliverance was mounted on a glossy horse, glaring. Stella turned the picture over. On the back was written, in faded ink: *D, Wormwood Mire.* Another photograph was of Aunt Temperance and Aunt Condolence, dressed in black, with pensive expressions, standing on either side of a draped urn. On the back, in the same writing: *T & C.*

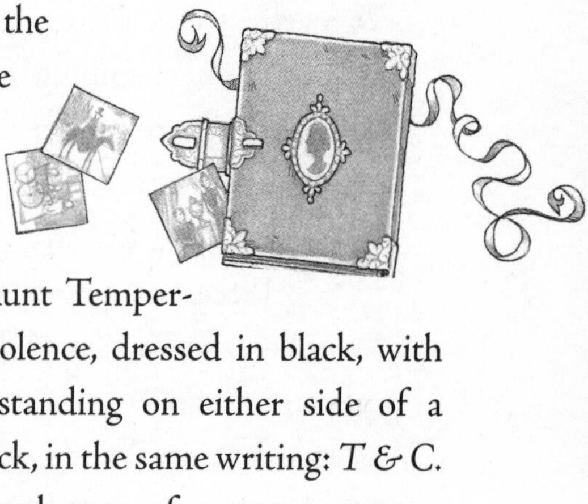

The third photograph was of a young woman in front of the same huge, dark house. Beside her was a perambulator containing two little children. They were all staring out of the picture with round, startled eyes. Stella turned the photograph over. She read, *P, S & L, Wormwood Mire.* She bit her finger. Her mother's name had been Patience. *P* could be for Patience. And *S* for Stella. Could she be one of the babies in the photograph? But then—

Footsteps tramped into the parlor, and Aunt Deliverance began to shout at someone. Stella jumped to her feet. She must not be found in the Aunts' bedroom. She slipped quickly into her own room, clutching the photograph.

Here the upheaval was even greater. Everything had been flung about. Her bed was upended, the bedclothes were torn, the mattress was slashed three or four times and feathers were spilling out. The washstand was overturned, the water jug smashed, the wardrobe doors were hanging open, and her clothes were ripped and strewn across the floor.

Pieces of paper were scattered everywhere. Stella gasped. It was the Atlas. It had been torn apart.

With shaking hands, she collected all the crumpled, wet pages and clutched them to her chest. The cover lay in a puddle under the washstand. She picked it up and bundled the pages back inside, looking desperately around for a safe hiding place.

The wardrobe had a cornice at the top, decorated with carved curlicues and bunches of grapes. Stella hauled the chair upright and shoved it across to the wardrobe. She climbed up. Standing on tiptoe, she reached as high as she could and pushed the bundled pages of the Atlas onto the top of the wardrobe, behind the cornice. It was safe for now, but it would certainly be found the next time the maids dusted. Tonight she must return it to the biscuit tin in the conservatory.

Her heart was thumping. This was the Professor's doing, she was sure of it. He must have made Ben look in the ink, and Ben had seen her hide the silver bottle under her mattress. And so the Professor had sent his men to get it. They had known where to search. But they had been too late, the bottle was not there anymore; it was safe in the little pocket around her neck.

A cold shiver ran down her back. She felt as if the Professor were looking over her shoulder. Almost as if he could hear her thoughts.

Twenty minutes later, still feeling shaken, Stella stood and watched the raindrops racing down the parlor window as the hotel servants put everything back in order, the Aunts took tea, and Mr. Fortescue, the owner of the hotel, was shouted at by Aunt Deliverance.

He was making little jerking bows and rubbing his hands together and saying, "Yes, madam. Of course, madam," and "I do apologize, madam."

A carpenter was fixing the lock, and Ada and Polly were busy setting the furniture straight. Four of the hotel housemaids heaved Stella's slashed mattress out through the parlor. Clumps of feathers escaped from its insides and drifted around the room.

Aunt Temperance made another squeaking noise and put a hand to her throat.

Aunt Condolence gasped, "Heavens."

Stella looked at the deep cuts in the mattress and shivered. What would the Professor do next? She pressed her hand against her chest, where Mr. Filbert's package was hidden. Would Ben tell the Professor where it was now? What should she do? She didn't want to tell the Aunts that she had spoken to Ben. They would be furious. But she knew she should. The Professor was just too dangerous.

"Aunt Deliverance—"

Aunt Deliverance stopped berating Mr. Fortescue long enough to snap, "Quiet, child."

"Please, I—"

All three Aunts turned and frowned at Stella.

"Children should be seen and not heard," said Aunt Temperance.

"But—"

"Quiet!" thundered Aunt Deliverance.

Stella opened her mouth, but before she could say anything, Aunt Deliverance said, "Do not speak until you are spoken to. Apply yourself to your needlework."

Stella picked up her sewing box from where it lay amongst the scattered contents of the writing desk and took it to the table, blinking back tears. She sat and started to untangle the silks, her fingers shaking.

The Aunts turned their furious glares back to Mr. Fortescue. Aunt Deliverance demanded that the police detectives return from London. Mr. Fortescue bowed and made agreeing noises.

Stella laid the silks in order and smoothed out the sampler. It was quite undamaged. She sighed, threaded a needle, and miserably started to sew.

The Aunts would be no help. She was on her own.

That night Stella sat on her unfamiliar new mattress, wrapped in her eiderdown, and put the pages of the Atlas back into order.

The Aunts had gone to bed and were snoring, but

the servants were still working. Stella could hear Ada scrubbing ink out of the carpet in the parlor. It was too early to venture out into the hotel, to find out what she could about Mr. Filbert and to hide the Atlas safely in the conservatory again.

In between the pages of the Atlas was the photograph of the woman and the two babies that had fallen from Aunt Temperance's album. Stella picked it up and gazed at it. They stared back at her. The little children looked identical, two pale faces with little strands of wispy hair escaping from their lace bonnets. Was it possible that she had been one of these babies? The woman in the photograph was small, and seemed somehow fragile and anxious. Her eyes were almost too large for her thin face. Stella turned it over and read, again, *P, S & L, Wormwood Mire*. If *S* was for Stella and *P* was Patience, her mother, then *L* had been—what—a sister, perhaps?

She propped the photograph up beside the candlestick and turned back to the Atlas. It was a sad bundle of crumpled, damp pages. She began to put them in order. *The fertile island of Zanzibar is famous for its cloves.* Stella carefully flattened out Zanzibar and wondered if the cloves in the rather nasty Military Pudding at luncheon had come from there. She smoothed out a torn map of New South Wales. "The emu has hairlike plumage and runs with extraordinary swiftness," she whispered to the woman and the two babies. They stared back at her, wide-eyed.

It was still raining. The Aunts snored. The clock in the parlor struck eleven, and then twelve. The candle burned down, flickering. At last Stella flattened the final page of the Atlas and placed the neat bundle of paper back inside the cover. She picked up the photograph, looked at it once more, and then tucked it between the pages. She tied the Atlas together like a parcel with a length of hair ribbon.

She climbed off the bed and put her ear to the door. Everything was quiet.

She pulled her thick felt dressing gown over her nightgown and put on her slippers. Mr. Filbert's package hung around her neck. She picked up the Atlas, blew out the candle, and unlocked the door with Ada's bedroom key.

It was quite dark. The Aunts were sleeping soundly.

She crept through their bedroom, opened the door to the parlor, and silently slipped through.

Twelve

The hotel was dark and quiet. Murmuring voices echoed from somewhere below. Stella felt uneasy. She crept along to the main staircase, leaned over cautiously, and looked down. Mr. Blenkinsop was at his desk, talking to one of the night footmen in a low voice. He pointed toward the front door, and the footman walked over to it and checked the lock.

Stella ducked behind the banister and retreated to the back staircase. She tiptoed down two flights of stairs and then along the shadowy second-floor passageway toward Mr. Filbert's room.

Ahead, soft footsteps approached. Stella froze, her heart thumping. A mildewy-looking stuffed fox stood on a small table. She dropped to her hands and knees, crawled underneath, and crouched in the

shadow, clutching the Atlas and holding her breath as the footsteps came closer.

It was one of the hotel porters. As still as a stone, Stella watched his boots march past. She waited until she could not hear his footsteps any longer, then crawled out from under the table and continued along to Mr. Filbert's room. The door was unlocked. She opened it, slipped inside, and closed it quietly behind her. The curtains were not drawn, and the dim light from the window was sufficient for her to see that the room was empty. The bed was stripped. There was nothing inside the wardrobe but curling shelf paper.

Stella stood in the deserted room and considered. Where could Mr. Filbert's luggage be? Perhaps the police had taken his things away? Or perhaps they had been locked in a storeroom somewhere?

She glanced at the Atlas, remembering she had found it, months ago, on the rubbish heap behind the hotel, beyond the kitchen garden. Perhaps when the maids had cleaned out Mr. Filbert's room, they had thrown some of his things there.

Stella opened the door and crept along the passageway to the stairs and down to the ground floor. She pushed open the baize door at the end of the passageway, slipped silently through, and tiptoed along to the kitchen. Her slippers made no sound on the tiled floor. The kitchen was huge and cavernous and dark. Rows of enormous, gleaming pots and pans dangled in the shadows overhead. Steam pipes hissed and clanked. The clock ticked, and a coal fire in one of the big ovens sputtered and popped.

Something touched her leg. She jumped. Two shining eyes looked up at her from the darkness. It was a kitchen cat. Stella stroked its arched back. 'Good evening, cat,' she whispered. The cat purred and butted its head against her leg.

She found candles and matches on a table. She lit a candle, set it in a brass holder, and tiptoed along the passageway, past the sculleries, to the garden door. The cat padded beside her. The door was bolted at the top and the bottom. The top bolt moved easily, but the lower one was stiff. Stella put down the candle and the Atlas and used both hands. The bolt moved with a shrill squeak and she froze, listening, fearing the noise had woken someone. But nothing stirred.

She picked up the candle and the Atlas and opened the door. The night outside was cold and dark and drizzling. On one side loomed the laundry building and on the other, the high wall of the kitchen garden.

Stella hesitated. The night was somehow larger

and darker than she had imagined it would be. Perhaps she should go back to bed. For a moment she thought she would. But it was unlikely she would have a chance to slip away during the daytime, with the Aunts so watchful and angry. And tomorrow the rubbish might be burned. Now was the only time.

She remembered poor Mr. Filbert lying dead in the conservatory. She took a deep breath, hugged the Atlas to her chest, gripped the candleholder firmly, and stepped out into the rain and the darkness.

The cat mewed in an interested manner and followed her out, along the path and through the gate in the garden wall.

The kitchen garden was full of dark shapes, winter plants muffled with straw and sacking. Beside the path was a row of tall brussels sprouts, like hunched old men, shrouded with burlap. Stella crept past them, and past dripping rows of leeks and rhubarb and cabbages. She ducked under a dangling dead flower head, the size of a fist.

Raindrops pattered on wet leaves. A shuffling sound came from somewhere nearby. She froze and peered into the darkness but could see nothing beyond the flickering circle of candlelight.

"Probably a fox," she whispered to the cat. She quickened her pace. At the far end of the kitchen

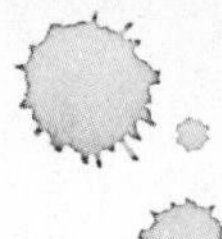

garden, behind a row of greenhouses, the rubbish heap was a piled dark shape, smelling strongly of wet horses and old vegetables. The candlelight revealed mounds of moldy straw, rags, a clump of rotting cabbage leaves, a broken wicker basket, and—

Stella gasped.

For a terrifying second, she thought a body lay sprawled on top of the rubbish heap. She held the candle higher, and her trembling hand made the flame flicker. It was the scarecrow she had seen lying in the entrance hall. She took two shaking steps closer. It was broken and coming to pieces. It lay on its back, its arms outflung and its neck arched, its face toward her. A trail of twigs and leaves showed where it had been dragged and flung onto the heap. For a moment she thought she saw the face move, the head lifting and turning. But it was only the candle's shifting light glistening on the wet, twisted sticks.

She took a deep breath and crouched down, holding the candle close to the figure's face. She could still make out the features, the cheekbones, nose, and chin. She remembered Mr. Filbert. His pale eyes and the way his skin seemed to stretch tightly across the bones of his face. Was this scarecrow poor Mr. Filbert? How could that be possible?

One of the scarecrow's hands was stretched

toward her, the fingers curled. Stella reached out, her heart thudding. As she touched it, the hand seemed to open, the twigs shifting and untwisting. She gasped and almost dropped the candle.

A loose twig lay in the scarecrow's palm. She picked it up and held it in the flickering candlelight. It was only a few inches long, and at the tip were several tiny unfurling leaves.

Shuffling footsteps made her stiffen, her heart in her throat. She pushed the little twig under the knot of the ribbon that tied the Atlas together and stood up.

Someone coughed.

Not a fox.

Perhaps one of the servants had woken and seen her candle.

She blew it out. The darkness closed in around her. She froze and listened. She could hear nothing but rain.

She had to force herself to move. Beyond the corner of the greenhouse, the wet brick path gleamed faintly. She took a deep breath and set off back across the garden, walking as quickly as she could.

Nearby, more footsteps. Stella turned and strained her eyes against the darkness and the steady drizzle. She could see nothing.

She continued across the garden, half running now. She was nearly there.

Suddenly the footsteps were close behind. She spun around and opened her mouth to scream. The beam from a lantern shone in her face, dazzling her.

A voice said, "It's her. It's the nipper." A thick blanket was dropped over her head, and rough hands snatched her off her feet. She twisted and struggled and tried to cry out.

The cat squawled.

A man cursed.

Stella tried to shout, but her mouth was full of hairy, horse-smelling blanket and she could not breathe. She felt dizzy and then everything seemed to spin around and disappear.

Thirteen

Stella awoke in darkness.

She was wet and cold and lying on her side on a hard surface, wrapped tightly in a rough, stinking blanket. It was difficult to breathe. There was a jolting movement and the sounds of wheels on cobblestones and a horse's hooves. Her arms and legs were pinned. She could feel a rope tied around her middle and around her ankles. She struggled but could barely move. She had never been more frightened in her life.

Close above her, a voice spoke in a hoarse whisper. "We'll take the nipper straight to the Professor?"

"That won't fadge. It's past midnight. He'll be snoozing at Flanagan's. We don't want to wake the whole ken."

"A golden strike, he said, Scuttler."

"I know, Charlie. We'll get the chink. We'll stash her someplace safe. Out of earshot. I ain't driving a cart around with a nipper tied up under the seat and the town crawling with flippin' peelers."

Her heart thumping, Stella recognized the voices. They were the two masked men who had been searching the hotel with the Professor the night Mr. Filbert had died. She remembered the whistling man she had seen when she and the Aunts had set off for their promenade. She had noticed his pale whiskers and his furtive look. He had seemed familiar, but she hadn't recognized him then. Now, too late, she realized he was one of the thieves.

They had been watching the hotel, and they had taken their chance to search her bedroom for Mr. Filbert's package. But they hadn't found it. So they had watched and waited for another opportunity. And she had walked right into their hands.

How could she have been so foolish?

"Where'll we stash her?"

The second voice said something that Stella didn't catch and chirruped to the horse. The harness clinked and the cart turned and then they were moving downhill. She could hear waves breaking on the shingle. Where were they taking her?

The cart lurched to a stop.

"Keep tout for the watchman."

"Old Joe? He'll be sleeping off that stingo."

After a moment there was a clink of keys and a creaking metallic noise, as if a gate was being opened. Stella was lifted up and carried. She struggled and tried to call out, but the hairy, muffling blanket made her choke.

"Stow that squeaking, girl."

She was roughly slung over a shoulder. She recognized the clanking sound of the turnstiles and then the men's footsteps clumping on the wooden boards of the pier. The blanket felt clammy and cold in the icy wind. After several minutes, keys jangled again and a door opened and then shut behind them. She was carried some distance up stairs, turning corners, up more stairs, and then another door was opened and she was dropped with a thump.

The rope was roughly untied and the blanket unwrapped and pulled away. She blinked, confused and dazzled by the lantern light. She was in a small room full of large objects, many of them wrapped in dust sheets. Faces stared from everywhere. A huge mask with round eyes and a lolling tongue goggled at her. An enormous painted sun leered and winked. A complicated-looking mechanical horse leaned against a pile of packing cases. She blinked again, her eyes stinging and her head swimming.

The two men loomed above her. She scrambled to her feet. "Wha-what do you want?"

"You've hid the Professor's gingabob," said the smaller man. "You tell us where you've stashed it, like a good little girl."

Stella tried to stop her voice from shaking. "When my Aunts find I'm missing, the police will come looking for me."

"You tell us where it is and we'll take you right back. You'll be snugabed and all's rug."

She shook her head. "I can't tell you."

"Cheese it with that rigmarole," he said. 'We're going to fetch the Professor. And you'll tell him where the little niggle thing is. Then Charlie and me will get our golden sovereign. Otherways you'll be nabbed in that muffler again and dropped in the sea, and nobody the wiser. Think on that, in the dark." He beckoned. "Come on, Charlie."

The door slammed shut, the key turned in the lock, and the footsteps tramped away.

Stella was alone.

She could feel all the fantastical creatures staring at her out of the darkness. She sank down onto the blanket and hugged her knees, shaking. This was awful. Did they really mean to tie her up and drop her in the sea? She imagined sinking down into the icy water. She did not want to drown.

And even if she gave them the silver bottle, would they let her go? The Professor had stabbed Mr. Filbert, just like that. He didn't mind killing people.

She clutched the little package that hung around her neck, under her dressing gown. Mr. Filbert had asked her to keep it safe, and she had promised she would. But how could she? The men would be back soon. The Professor would be with them. And then he would take it from her, and there was nothing she could do about it.

Her eyes filled with tears.

The Aunts would not know she was gone until they found her bed empty in the morning. And that was hours away. There was no help coming. She was on her own.

Tears trickled down her face. She shivered and reached out in the darkness for the blanket. Her hand touched something familiar. It was the Atlas. It had been captured along with her. She picked it up and hugged it to her chest. It felt comforting and smelled of mildew and old wet paper. As she stroked its cover, she felt braver. She sniffed and wiped her eyes. There must be something she could do.

Her eyes were becoming accustomed to the

darkness. She realized she could make out indistinct shapes. She could see the outline of the door.

She got to her feet and felt her way over to it. She groped for the handle and turned it back and forth uselessly. It was locked.

She looked around. High up on the opposite wall, a paler rectangle gleamed faintly. A window? Stella felt her way across the room, groped around, and found a wooden packing case. She put her knee on it, climbed up, and then up again onto another case. She reached up to the window, felt around for the latch, and shoved it open.

Dim light filtered into the room. Stella heaved herself up and poked her head out of the window. The night was cold, but the rain had stopped and the moon shone from behind ragged clouds. Looking to the left, she could see nothing but darkness, but to the right she could see the gaslights on the pier and the twinkling lights of Withering-by-Sea.

She was in the theater. She had often gazed at it from the Front, admiring its white domes and colorful fluttering flags. It perched right at the end of the pier, over the sea. She had longed to visit it. And now she was locked up inside it.

The little window was high up on one side of the theater. It was small, but perhaps she could wriggle through it. But then what? She leaned farther out and looked down. A long way below, dark waves frothed around the pier's spindly legs. The water looked black and cold. Stella swallowed and clutched the windowsill, feeling dizzy.

Twenty feet below her, just above the water, was a narrow iron walkway. It was draped with seaweed and looked extremely slippery. Could she climb out of the window and let herself down with a rope? If she slipped or let go of the rope, she would be in the water, and she could not swim. She watched a large wave break over the walkway in a purposeful manner, and her stomach lurched.

She withdrew from the window and climbed back down. She found the rope the men had tied her up with and measured it out with her hands. It would not be long enough.

She picked up the Atlas again and hugged it. The moonlight was too dim to read by, which was a pity because the Atlas was always encouraging. She remembered the

page with the map of North America. On it was a picture of a creature with a pointed nose, a curling tail, and many sharp-looking teeth. *The opossum is a most crafty animal, and when beset by pursuers, frequently deceives its foe and quietly makes its escape.*

She would be crafty. As crafty as an opossum.

She coiled the rope and climbed back up to the window. She tied one end of the rope firmly around the window latch and pushed the rest out, letting it dangle outside. The end of the rope hung some distance above the walkway.

She climbed back down into the room, picked up the Atlas, and crept behind the horrible mask with the goggling eyes. She pulled back the edge of a dust sheet. It was covering a large papier-mâché elephant on a kind of trolley. There was room to hide beneath the trolley, between the wheels. Clutching the Atlas, Stella wriggled her way underneath and let the dust sheet drop behind her. She was quite hidden.

She settled down to wait.

Fourteen

Stella lay in the dark with her cheek pressed to the dusty wooden floor. She could hear the sea outside and creaks and groans throughout the building. It was very cold. Despite her dressing gown and slippers, she shivered. Her feet were like ice. Several times she thought she heard footsteps or voices or distant wailing music. But nobody came. She began to drift off to sleep.

She awoke with a jolt when a key turned in the lock and the door opened.

"We put the nipper in here, Professor."

"Excellent," said the quiet voice that Stella remembered. Lantern light gleamed through the dust sheet. She held her breath.

"Where—"

"Cop that! She's piked out the glaze."

The light flickered, and footsteps trod heavily across the room. It sounded as if someone was climbing up on the packing cases. There was a crash, then splintering wood and scrambling noises and some cursing.

"Me flippin' leg."

"She's bleedin' got out the window and gone down a rope. There's an iron jake down there."

"You have allowed her to escape." The quiet voice was furious.

"I didn't smoke that there little window, Professor."

"You've bungled again. Quickly—you, come with me. Bring that blanket. She will not slip through my hands again. You, get the others. And fetch the boy."

There were scuffling noises, the door banged, the footsteps tramped away, and the room was again in darkness. Stella lay still and counted slowly to ten. And then to twenty, just to be sure the men had gone.

She lifted the dust sheet and wriggled back out from underneath the elephant's trolley. Her legs were frozen and shaky. She crept around the goggling mask and tiptoed to the door. It was unlocked. Outside, a dusty passage, lined with doors and papered with playbills, stretched away into darkness. She slipped out of the room, closed the door behind her, and crept along the passage. At the end, a winding wooden staircase led down. She could hear the building creaking and the distant sounds of the sea.

At the foot of the stairs was a cavernous room. Pipes and valves and machinery loomed out of the darkness. She threaded her way between a complicated series of ropes and pulleys and an enormous mechanical sea monster and found another staircase beyond.

She climbed up and up, ducking beneath a wooden beam and several ropes and dangling sandbags. She opened a narrow door and was startled to find herself out on a balcony, with the empty stage and hundreds of red plush seats in rows below, and arches and gilt angels and stars above.

It was beautiful. Pale moonlight shone through the colored glass windows in a dome in the center of the ceiling. Marble columns, swags of golden flowers, fat cherubs, and curling brass gas brackets gleamed in the shadows. The smells of cigar smoke and orange peel hung in the air.

Stella tiptoed along the curving balcony and pushed open a swinging door. Marble arches and pillars branched upward and a wide staircase led down. She peeped around a marble lady who stood at the head of the stairs, holding a gas lamp. Below, moonlight shone in through the glass entrance doors onto the patterned mosaic floor. *The way out.* Stella started down the stairs.

Suddenly voices echoed, lantern light flickered, and the glass doors swung open. The Professor strode in, followed by four or five other men. Stella darted back up the stairs and crouched behind the marble lady, her heart thumping.

The Professor was speaking. His voice was controlled and furious. "... fooled by a child. A girl. That rope hung well short of the walkway—it was a blind. And you imbeciles fell for it."

Someone sneezed, and a voice mumbled, "Flippin' well fell right in the sea, didn't I?"

Cautiously Stella looked out from her hiding place. She saw the Professor whip around and lash out with his cane. There was a yelp. "Your own fault, you fool. And where is the boy?"

There was a muffled answer and the Professor snapped, "Run away? He can't have got far. Go after him. Find him and bring him to me. Do you have the box?"

One of the men stepped forward. He held out a small box made of inlaid wood and brass. The Professor unlocked it with a key from his watch chain and opened it up. Stella leaned farther out from

behind the marble lady and peered down. The box was lined with blue velvet. The Professor reached inside and took out something small and dark and metallic. It looked like a black beetle.

He took a silver screwdriver from the box, inserted it into the beetle, and twisted. *Click.* The glossy shell of the beetle opened and revealed gleaming clockwork inside.

"The blanket," he said, snapping his fingers.

A man came forward. He held out the gray blanket Stella had been wrapped in. The Professor returned the screwdriver to the box and took out a pair of silver tweezers. He beckoned the man holding the lantern to bring it closer. His green-tinted spectacles glinted in the light as he inspected the blanket.

"Yes," he said, and picked something from its surface, using the tweezers. "Yes."

A strand of pale hair gleamed in the lantern light. The Professor coiled the hair and placed it into the interior of the beetle and closed the shell with a click. Then he returned the tweezers to the box and took a silver key.

"Undoubtedly she is concealed somewhere in the theater." He inserted the key into the beetle and started to turn it, as if winding a watch. "I will remain here and watch this door and the stage door. There is no other way out. She cannot escape." He replaced the key in the box.

The beetle's wings snapped open. It emitted a rattling buzz, took flight, and hovered several inches above his palm.

"If she is hiding, this will find her," he said. "Follow it."

The beetle flew in a circle, as if taking a scent from the air. It circled again. Its flight was uneven but purposeful. It hovered for a moment and then turned decisively in the direction of the staircase.

Stella fled.

She pushed through the swinging doors into the auditorium. She sprinted along the balcony, through the door at the end, and headlong down the dark staircase.

At the foot of the stairs, she found herself again in the cavernous room underneath the stage that was full of ropes and machinery. She could hear the beetle's buzzing close behind, and the men's voices and tramping feet following.

She dashed across the shadowy room, ducking between the looming obstacles and behind the enormous mechanical sea monster. A wooden ladder against the wall led upward. She darted over and climbed it, as quickly and silently as she could, clutching the Atlas awkwardly to her chest. At the top, a narrow, unstable walkway wound between ropes and pulleys. Below, she could hear thumping noises, cursing, and a loud sneeze. She looked down and saw the lantern swinging wildly, and shadowy figures stumbling around.

She crept along the walkway and found another ladder. She climbed down and pushed open a door into a dark passageway.

She heard the buzzing noise again, sudden and close. She gasped and ducked. The beetle skimmed past her ear.

She tried a door. It was locked. She darted to the next one and rattled the handle. It was locked too, and so was the next. The beetle flew hard into the side of her head. She yelped and batted it away with the Atlas.

Gasping, she dashed to the next door and turned the handle. It opened. Too late, she saw a light shining and heard someone snoring. She hesitated. The beetle banged into her cheek. Panicky, she swatted wildly at it. It flew into her face again. She swung the Atlas and knocked it away. It collided with the wall and fell to the floor. The buzzing faltered and stopped.

She darted into the room and closed the door silently behind her. She stood with her back to it, panting.

A lamp glowed and a coal fire hissed in a small grate. Woven baskets and empty cages were stacked in piles. There was a strong smell of fish. A man was sleeping in a chair. He was small and fat, with a curled black mustache. His shirt was unbuttoned at the neck. His suspenders were embroidered with roses. There was a rug over his knees, and on the rug slept an enormous tabby cat. A black-and-white cat lay across the man's shoulders, and another cat sprawled on a small table beside a violin. Everywhere Stella looked there were sleeping cats. The sound of their purring filled the room.

In the passageway outside, she heard buzzing start up again. Her heart sank. It started and stopped several times, then started determinedly. The beetle flew hard against the door. *Knock, knock.*

The sleeping man woke up with a snort. He rubbed his eyes. "Eh? What? *Avanti.* Who is there? Come in."

The beetle collided with the door again. *Knock, knock, knock.*

Stella ducked behind a screen that stood in a corner, concealing a small washstand. She put her eye to a gap in the screen where the hinges met.

Knock, knock, knock.

Fifteen

Knock, knock, knock.

Behind the screen, Stella held her breath.

The man called "Come in" again. He muttered something, pushed the cat off his lap, lifted the second cat from his shoulders, and stood up. "Yes, yes. I am coming."

He opened the door. The beetle flew into the room and banged against a cage. A cat swiped at it.

"Gastone!" said the man. "*Attento!* What is it? Be most careful! It is a frightful insect!"

The beetle flew in a lopsided circle, buzzing erratically. The man flapped his hands at it and knocked a cage over. It crashed to the floor, startling the cats. A small gray cat jumped high and batted at the beetle as it flew past. A ginger cat leaped from the top of a basket to the mantelpiece, knocking off several dishes and a tin mug, and stood, poised to jump, lashing its tail. Several cats hissed loudly. The huge tabby sprang into the air from the back of the chair, paws outstretched.

"No, Alfredo! No!" cried the man, waving his arms. Two more cages toppled over.

The cat knocked the beetle out of the air. The beetle hit the ground. The cat landed beside it, picked the beetle up in its mouth, and started to chew, with a thoughtful expression.

"Alfredo! Drop it! *Cattivo!*" said the man. He clasped the big cat in his arms and prized open its mouth. The beetle fell out onto the floor. It gave a wavering, buzzing rattle and lay still. The man peered at it. He put the cat down and poked the beetle with his finger. The shell clicked open, and several tiny pieces of clockwork fell out.

The man muttered, "*Molto strano*," and gingerly picked up the beetle. He peered into its insides. He extracted the strand of hair, held it between his thumb and finger thoughtfully for a moment, and then put it into the fire.

He placed the beetle on the mantelpiece, shut the door, and began to pick up the fallen cages and tidy the room, talking to the cats in a calming, sing-song voice in a foreign language. Not French, Stella thought. Even more foreign than French.

He sat back in his chair, shook out the rug, and laid it over his knees again. He seized a black bottle from the table beside him, pulled out the cork with his teeth, and took a swig. The big tabby cat jumped up into his lap, turned around twice, and started to wash its paws. The black-and-white cat sprawled across his shoulders once more.

The man thrust the cork back into the bottle, clasped his hands over his belly, and closed his eyes.

Before Stella could move, there was a loud thump outside in the passageway, followed by muffled cursing and a sneeze. The door handle rattled and the door banged open.

Two men strode into the room. Stella recognized her kidnappers, Scuttler and Charlie. Two more men crowded in behind them. One was limping, and the other was shivering and dripping, wrapped in the hairy gray blanket. He sneezed miserably.

The fat man rubbed his eyes and exclaimed in a foreign language.

"Mr. Capelli." Scuttler sounded surprised.

The fat man sat up in the chair, careful not to disturb the cats, and said, "Why are you awaking me?"

"Didn't know you was in here."

"My Alfredo, I think he is *indisposto,* unwell," said the fat man, stroking the cat on his lap. It opened its green eyes and stared at the intruders. "So I sit with him tonight. But no, I think he has—what is the word—*malata di nostalgia?* So I feed him a herring, and all is good."

Scuttler said, "We're looking for a buzzbug. A beetle." His gaze darted around the room.

Behind the screen, Stella froze.

"Yes, the insect is here. It is already awaking me. It is a most dreadful creature. It would certainly be injuring my cats!" He pointed at the mantelpiece, where the beetle lay.

"Cripes. The Professor'll be spittin' blue murder," said Charlie. He went over and poked the beetle. It gave a short, rattling buzz, and he jumped nervously.

"It is attacking my cats. It was most frightful."

"Maybe that was a cat hair he put in it, accidental," said Scuttler. "So it went chasing after cats instead of the nipper. Give it here, Charlie."

Charlie passed him the beetle, and Scuttler took it gingerly between a finger and thumb and peered into it. "There ain't no hair in it now, at any rate." He shrugged and wrapped it in a grimy handkerchief and pushed it into his pocket. "We're looking for a nipper. A little girl," he said, turning to the fat man.

"There is nobody here." He shook his head. "As you can see. Only me and my cats."

Charlie came farther into the room. He held the lantern aloft and peered behind a stack of cages. Stella watched him approach, her heart thumping.

A ginger cat, lying on top of the cages, hissed at him. "Nice puss," he said nervously. The cat lashed out with a paw. He jumped back. "Flippin' heck!"

"Gastone! No!" said the fat man, looking agitated. "You must go. You are most disturbing to my cats. There is nobody here."

"It's for the Professor. The nipper stole something off him." He sucked his hand where the cat had scratched him. "She's skrivin' somewhere."

"She is not here," said the fat man firmly.

"Like he says, it's for the Professor. We got to search the whole ken." Scuttler looked apprehensively at the angry cat. It flattened its ears against its head and hissed again. Another cat yowled and swiped a paw at the wet man in the blanket. He shrank back. A cat jumped up onto a basket and made a sound like steam escaping from a kettle. The men flinched.

"Gastone! Flora! Giorgio!" the fat man cried. "Truly, you must depart. You can see there is no child here."

The men backed away nervously from the angry cats. Scuttler said, "Well, Mr. Capelli. Keep your oglers open."

"Yes, yes."

They gave one final glance around the room, then turned and left, slamming the door behind them. Their footsteps tramped away.

The fat man spoke in his calming voice, in the foreign language, and stroked all the cats within reach. One by one, they settled down and started to purr. The man leaned back in his chair and took another swig from the black bottle. He sighed and closed his eyes.

Stella watched until the man and all the cats seemed to be sleeping. She waited several more minutes. When everything was quite still, she crept out from behind the screen and tiptoed toward the door.

She put her ear to it and listened. There were voices and footsteps not far away. A door slammed and someone sneezed. Cautiously, she turned the handle.

A movement behind her made her jump. She

turned and saw that the fat man was awake. He smiled. "Wait," he whispered.

He put a finger to his lips. Stella hesitated, hugging the Atlas to her chest.

He gently removed the sleeping cats and stood up. He went to the door and listened, his head to one side. Then he opened it, and he and Stella looked out into the darkness.

After a moment he whispered, "They have gone away. They are out of hearing. They will not come back, I think. You are quite safe." He closed the door again and turned the key. He smiled at her. "I am Otto Capelli," he said. "This is Alfredo." He pointed to the big tabby cat sitting on the chair. Alfredo yawned and stared peacefully at Stella through half-closed eyes. "Violetta." He indicated the black-and-white cat. "Annina, Gastone, Flora"—he pointed to the seven cats one by one—"and Giorgio and little Guiseppe." The cats wore beautiful leather collars with their names stamped in gold. Mr. Capelli spread out his hands with a flourish and bowed. "Signor Capelli's Educated Cats. We are most famous, yes?"

Stella thought she had seen his name on a poster at the entrance to the pier, and so she nodded. "I'm—my name is Stella Montgomery," she said. She put out a hand to Guiseppe, a smallish gray cat perched on top of a basket. He touched her finger with his nose, blinked at her, and purred. She stroked his soft fur.

"Stella. It means 'star.' You know this?" asked Mr. Capelli.

Stella shook her head.

"Yes, yes," he said. "In my language. Yes. My cats like you. That is good."

"They are lovely," she said. It was true. The cats were plump, with glossy fur and alert expressions.

"Yes, yes. They are most beautiful. And they are artistes." He picked up the violin. "See." He plucked a couple of the strings. All the cats turned their heads toward him and looked attentive.

He took the bow and started to play a strange, wild, wailing tune. The cats sat up straight and watched him, ears pricked.

Mr. Capelli smiled at them and nodded.

The cats opened their mouths and began to sing.

Sixteen

The cats' singing was the strangest sound, a yowling accompaniment to the violin's melody, rising and falling in chorus. Mr. Capelli smiled and nodded and swayed from side to side as he played. His bow skipped across the strings, and his fingers danced. Every now and then, one cat sang higher or louder or longer and Mr. Capelli said, "*Sì*, Alfredo. Yes, yes. Good, Gastone. Very good. Yes, Annina, *bella mia*."

Stella thought it was somewhat like the sound of

a steam organ with many different wailing, wheezing pipes. It was strange and quite beautiful.

The song rose to a high keening note and then died away.

Stella clapped.

Mr. Capelli beamed as he laid down the violin. "My cats are artistes, yes?" He stroked the cats and said something to each of them. They looked lovingly into his face.

"H-how do you teach them?" Stella asked.

He held up three fingers and counted. "Kindness. Patience. Fish." He threw a cushion onto the hearth-rug and waved a welcoming hand at it. "Come, sit here. It is warm."

Stella hesitated. Alfredo, the enormous tabby, jumped down onto the rug. He arched his back, stretched, and lay down next to the cushion. He blinked welcomingly at her. She went over and sat down beside him. Flora, a smaller tortoiseshell cat with round orange eyes, came toward her, purring. Stella stroked them both. The coal fire hissed. It was very agreeable to feel warm.

Mr. Capelli took an enamel mug from the mantelpiece, poured some of the contents of the black bottle into it, and offered it to her.

"Thank you," she said. It smelled powerfully of

orange peel and herbs. She tasted it doubtfully. It burned her mouth and her throat, but it warmed her insides.

"What is it?" she asked. She took another sip.

"A most splendid tonic." Mr. Capelli sat back down in his chair and took a swig from the bottle. "It is most healthy for the stomach. It is from my home. The island of San Marco. You will not have heard of it."

"Well, yes, I think . . ." Stella untied the ribbon from the Atlas and searched through the loose pages. San Marco was one of a handful of islands scattered across a blue sea. In the margin, there was a picture of a ruined tower on a rocky hill above a harbor. She read aloud, "Olives, oranges, figs, and pomegranates are grown, and abundant grapes, which are made both into wine and raisins."

She passed the page to Mr. Capelli. He looked at the map of the little island and his eyes sparkled. "Here is my home." He pointed. "One day, when we are rich, we will return and buy a farm. My cats and I will sit in the sun. It is most dreadfully cold in this country. Too cold for me. Too cold for my cats." He passed the page back to Stella.

She looked at the picture. "It's beautiful," she said.

"Yes." He wiped his eyes and took another drink.

After a moment he said, "So, Stella Montgomery." He gestured expansively with the bottle. "Tell me everything."

Stella said, "I need to get away from here. I need to get home. But the Professor is watching the front of the theater. Is there another way out?"

Mr. Capelli shook his head. "Unless you can swim."

Stella shivered, remembering the black, icy waves.

"*Bene*. So. These men, they are looking for you. They will not find you. And then, perhaps, they will leave." Mr. Capelli gestured, as if flinging something away. "You will stay here, where it is safe. We will wait, and then I will go and see. And you are hungry, yes?"

Stella realized she was extremely hungry. She nodded.

"I have toast and butter. And a splendid herring." He opened a small cupboard and pulled out a loaf of bread, a lump of butter wrapped in paper, and a smoked herring. He cut a piece of bread and passed it to Stella with a toasting fork. She threaded the bread carefully onto the fork and held it over the coals.

He fed little pieces of fish to the cats. He said seriously, "I do not like the Professor. He is most frightful. I will not—what is the word? I will not betray you to him. But stealing from him, it is wrong, and it is most dangerous."

"No, no. I didn't steal anything. It wasn't like that at all." Stella looked at Mr. Capelli. Should she tell him about Mr. Filbert? She thought she could trust him. Perhaps he could help. She inspected the bread and turned it over. She said, "Someone, a gentleman, asked me to look after something. To keep it safe. And I promised. But the Professor wants it." She hesitated, and then put down the toasting fork, pulled out the little pocket from beneath her dressing gown, and unwrapped Mr. Filbert's little silver bottle. "Look," she said.

Mr. Capelli took it from her "What is it?" he asked, turning it over in his hands. "What is inside?"

There was a faint slithering sound, something moved inside the bottle, and dark shadows flickered and swam across the walls. One of the cats hissed suddenly, and Stella jumped.

"I don't know," she said. "I think it's something magic, from the olden days."

He studied it for a moment, his head to one side. "It is very old," he said. He handed it back to her. She wrapped it up, returned it to the pocket, and picked up the toasting fork again.

"If I don't get home tonight, my Aunts will be very angry."

"You have many Aunts?" he asked.

"Three. They live in the Hotel Majestic. Up on the cliff. Those men brought me here. But I escaped from them. The Professor's beetle was chasing me. The Professor put my hair inside it and it came after me."

"Never, never leave your hair. Or your—what is the word?"—he pointed to his fingernails—"these cuttings, anywhere. It is not safe, not at all. Me, I always burn them. And blood, of course, is the most dangerous of all. So, this gentleman. What of him?"

"He is dead."

Mr. Capelli froze with his bottle halfway to his lips. "*Gran Dio!* Dead?"

Stella nodded. "Yes. The Professor stabbed him. He stabbed him!"

"Tell me everything, from the start," said Mr. Capelli.

Stella thought for a moment, putting things in order, and then she told him the whole story. Everything that had happened, from when she had first seen Mr. Filbert hide the little package in the Chinese urn in the conservatory.

Mr. Capelli listened without interrupting. When she had finished, he said, "The Professor stabbed the gentleman. And then the gentleman turned into sticks?"

Stella nodded. "Yes. I think so." She remembered the little twig. "See?" She took it from the ribbon that held the Atlas together and held it out to him.

"The gentleman turned into sticks," repeated Mr. Capelli thoughtfully, holding the twig in the light of the lamp. "This is *nocciolo*. What is the word? Hazelwood." He smiled at Stella. "If you plant this in the ground, it will grow into a hazel tree. In time." He passed the twig back to her. "When I was a boy, my *nonna*, my grandmother, told me stories of trees. We would leave gifts, almond cakes and wine, in May and at midsummer. For the spirits who lived within the trees, you understand. And if you cut a tree, an oak or an elm or a cypress, you would ask the spirit first. It is dangerous to cut a tree without asking."

As he spoke, he took the toast from Stella, buttered it, laid a piece of smoked herring on top, and passed it back.

She took a bite. It was salty and crispy and delicious. She threaded another slice of bread onto the toasting fork and held it over the fire.

Mr. Capelli said, "The hazel trees were for protection. Tie two twigs together"—he gestured with his fingers—"like this, in a cross, with red thread and nail it above the door, and the house is protected from lightning. Put a twig in your shoe, yes? You will have a safe journey, protected from witches. A baby's cradle is made from hazelwood, and the baby is protected from the *folletti*, the fairies. And if you have a treasure, you might bury it under a hazel tree. The spirit in the tree, he will protect your treasure."

"Did you see the spirits? What were they like?"

"No, no. This is not now. This was many, many years ago. Now they are all gone. Or perhaps sleeping like old men and women. But on San Marco, we remember them, although they are no longer there." He shrugged. "My *nonna* told me of when she was a little girl. And there was a man in her village, his grandmother was an elm tree. My *nonna* knew him when he was very, very old. He lived a hundred years. And when he died and he was laid in the church, he changed into wood. Into an old, old branch of an elm tree."

Stella looked into the fire and thought about Mr. Filbert. Could he have been the spirit of a tree? Of a hazel tree? She tried to remember exactly what Ben had said about the Professor cutting down a tree at night and digging underneath. Had the silver bottle been hidden under a hazel tree?

"The Professor called him Dryad," she said, remembering.

"That is a name for a tree spirit." Mr. Capelli

nodded. "They have many names. That one is from the Greeks. From the very ancient times. Many, many years ago. Then, they say, the tree spirits were tall and strong, and people were fearful. But now the old ones, the *folletti,* have faded away, and instead we have the modern world of factories and steam engines and the telegraph."

Stella remembered Mr. Filbert. How very old he had been. How his fingers had been like dry twigs, his skin had seemed almost green, and when she had touched his face, it had felt rough, like the bark of a tree.

She blinked. She smelled smoke. The toast was burning. She must have closed her eyes for a moment. "Oh no! I'm so sorry, Mr. Capelli."

He laughed. "It is not so dreadful." He spread the blackened toast with butter and crunched into it. "It has more taste. And you are tired. It is most frightfully late." He jumped up from the chair and bustled about the room, collecting an armful of cushions and rugs. "You will be splendid here, behind the screen? Then, if we are disturbed, you are hidden." He laid the cushions together and shook out a red tartan rug.

"You prepare yourself for sleep. I will go and see if the Professor is still there. I will lock the door. You will be quite safe."

"Thank you, Mr. Capelli," she said. She felt so tired she could hardly keep her eyes open. She stumbled across to the washstand, splashed some water onto her face, and yawned. Shrugging off her dressing gown and slippers, she lay down on the cushions and pulled the rug over herself. Alfredo stalked across the top of her, turned around twice, and curled up in the crook of her knees, purring. Another cat joined them, and a third.

Stella thought about the Aunts. In the morning they would find her gone. But there was nothing she could do about that. She was very sleepy. She shut her eyes.

When Mr. Capelli came back into the room, she was almost asleep.

"The Professor is still there, but he did not see me," he said. "He is watching the front of the theater. The main door and the stage door. But you are safe here."

Stella imagined the Professor's tall figure and gaunt yellow face. Watching and waiting.

She curled up and hugged the Atlas to her chest. She dropped into sleep, warm and safe, surrounded by purring cats.

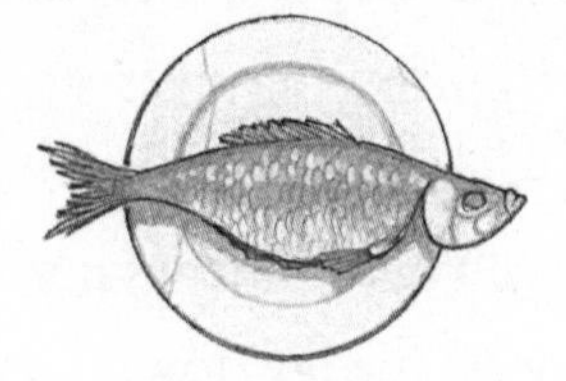

Seventeen

Stella awoke in daylight, and for a moment she did not remember where she was. Then she smelled toast and heard someone humming a tune. She pushed back the rug, wriggled out from underneath a couple of sleeping cats, and sat up.

The humming stopped. "You are awake." Mr. Capelli poked his head around the screen. He held the toasting fork in one hand and a herring in the other. Alfredo lay across his shoulders, his green eyes fixed on the herring.

"Good morning," said Stella. She rubbed her eyes and yawned.

"Yes, yes. Good morning," said Mr. Capelli. "Or good afternoon, perhaps? You sleep well?"

"What time is it?" asked Stella, horrified. She

scrambled to her feet and looked around for her dressing gown and slippers.

Mr. Capelli disappeared for a moment, then appeared again, without the herring but holding a watch. "It is nearly one o'clock. You sleep for many, many hours." Alfredo jumped from his shoulders and shot out of sight. "No, Alfredo. No! *Cattivo!*" Mr. Capelli disappeared again, and there was some scuffling and an annoyed mew. He appeared, beaming, with the herring clutched to his chest. "I put it down for one second only," he said. "But always he watches me. He is most clever. And most naughty." He waggled a finger at Alfredo. "No fish for you! Well, perhaps a tiny bit. There." He broke off a generous piece of the herring, gave it to Alfredo, and stroked the cat's head.

He turned to Stella. "I will show you the water closet. And we will eat."

"But—" Stella started to say.

"The Professor is still watching," said Mr. Capelli, feeding pieces of fish to other cats. "I take my cats out for a walk early, for milk. And he is there, at the front of the theater. And those men, they follow me. They are most suspicious. And later, I creep down and spy and he is still watching. A mouse could not escape!"

"Still watching?" Stella's heart sank. "Oh no."

"Yes, yes, it is most frightful. But I have a splendid

plan," Mr. Capelli waved the toasting fork at Stella. "And I will tell you it while we eat."

She pulled on her dressing gown and slippers. Mr. Capelli opened the door a crack and looked out. Stella could hear footsteps and voices and someone playing a pianoforte and laughing. Mr. Capelli beckoned to her and pointed to a door at the end of the passage.

"That is the water closet," he said.

It was tiny, filthy, and extremely cold. Gusts of icy sea air blew in through the gaps between the floorboards. Looking down the lavatory, Stella was startled to find it open to the sea. A long way below, grayish-green waves surged and frothed. A large, dark fish swam past.

She used the lavatory quickly, pulled the heavy iron lever (starting a disconcerting series of clanks and bangs and trickling noises), and hurried back to the warmth of Mr. Capelli's dressing room.

"You will have toast, yes?" he said. "And milk." He passed her a piece of toast and herring and a mug of milk. He poured milk into a bowl and placed it on the hearthrug. The cats clustered around to lap. Mr. Capelli smiled at them fondly and took a swig from his black bottle.

"So," he said. "You know, we have a big splendid show today, at two o'clock? A matinee. And the

Professor also is performing. And all those men, they work in the theater. They will be busy, busy pulling ropes and working the limelights, yes?"

Her mouth full, Stella could only nod.

Mr. Capelli gestured expansively. "So, it is easy. You can escape then. While the Professor is busy, and all those men are working, and everyone is watching the show, and there are many, many people everywhere. I will show you the stage door. It is to the side of the main door. That will be the best way."

But would the Professor be expecting that? Would he have made a plan? Stella swallowed. She said, "Thank you, Mr. Capelli," and tried to ignore the nervous feeling in her insides.

"It is nothing," Mr. Capelli said, beaming. "It is less than nothing." He picked up a brush from the mantelpiece, scooped up Violetta, and sat down on the chair. "So, you will return to your Aunts?" he asked as he began to groom the cat.

Stella took another brush. She knelt beside Alfredo on the hearthrug and stroked the brush along his back. "Yes," she said. Her heart sank when she thought of the Aunts and how angry they would be. "And I will talk to the police detectives about the Professor, if I can. If they will listen to me."

"So, you will go straight back to the hotel. To your

Aunts and the policemen," said Mr. Capelli. "Splendid. You will be safe."

"I hope so," said Stella.

"And what will you do with that thing?" Mr. Capelli gestured toward where Mr. Filbert's package was hidden, hanging around her neck.

"I don't know," she said. She wished she knew what the mysterious silver bottle was. Something very precious that someone had buried under the ancient hazel tree for safekeeping. But what? It was no good just running and hiding. She needed to make a plan. She tried to think while she helped to groom the cats, but it was difficult to concentrate. Alfredo rolled over onto his back. Annina pounced on his tail and bit it. He gave an angry mew and scrambled up onto Mr. Capelli's shoulder and hissed at her, his ears flat on his head. Mr. Capelli laughed and patted him. Stella started brushing Annina. The cat squirmed and tried to bite the brush. Despite her worries, Stella giggled.

"They are excited," said Mr. Capelli. "They are most splendid artistes. They have temperament, you understand."

At last, when all the cats were smooth and glossy (and Stella had been scratched three times and bitten once and was covered with cat fur), Mr. Capelli went behind the screen to change into his costume. Stella removed the cats' leather collars and replaced them with fancy collars embroidered with gold thread and sequins. The cats were making a lot of noise, wailing and yowling.

"They practice," said Mr. Capelli from behind the screen. "They get ready to perform." He started to sing, and the cats joined in enthusiastically, lifting their heads and swaying from side to side.

There was a knock at the door. Stella jumped. Before she could duck out of sight, the door opened and a boy's head poked into the room. He snatched off his cap. "Fifteen minutes, Mr. Capelli, sir."

"*Sì, sì.* Thank you!" shouted Mr. Capelli.

The boy glanced at Stella. His eyes widened, and then the door slammed and his footsteps hurried away.

"He saw me," gasped Stella, her heart thumping.

"Yes," said Mr. Capelli.

"He'll tell the Professor."

"Yes, perhaps. But it is not so dreadful." Mr. Capelli emerged from behind the screen. He wore a red-spangled coat and a sparkling red-and-gold waistcoat. His mustache was curled and shiny. He placed a glossy black top hat on his head. He looked magnificent. "Because now, very fast, we go. I will show you the stage door. Where you can escape straightaway, I think." He attached leads to the cats' collars. He tucked the violin under his arm. Alfredo leaped up onto his shoulder. "Come," he said, and opened the door.

Stella picked up the Atlas and followed him.

Outside in the passage, three men in striped bathing costumes with bristling military mustaches were performing vigorous exercises and shouting "*Hup, hup.*" A tall lady stalked past, dressed entirely in pink feathers with an enormous nodding plume on top of her head.

Mr. Capelli walked quickly along the passage, Alfredo perched on his shoulder and the other cats trotting beside him, their tails pointing straight up in the air. Stella hurried along behind, keeping her head down and trying to escape attention. But it was difficult not to stare. There were remarkable things to see on every side.

At the top of the stairs, four or five dark-eyed children, some of them even smaller than Stella, were bending and stretching in an astonishing manner. A girl took hold of a little boy and bent him over backward into the shape of a croquet hoop. He grinned at Stella from between his own ankles. Stella smiled back nervously.

At the bottom of the stairs, a man led a small donkey past them. A woman was singing trills, higher and higher. An enormous man with bulging muscles, wearing a tiger skin, cried *"Alley oop!"* and upended himself against a wall, his hands on the ground and his feet in the air. Stella gaped at him. He winked at her, upside down.

People greeted Mr. Capelli and he answered them, but he did not stop.

They passed a group of dancers in mermaid costumes, chattering and practicing fancy steps. Stella glanced behind and saw the boy with the cap threading his way through the crowd.

"Look!" she gasped.

"This way," said Mr. Capelli decisively. He squeezed quickly between the dancers and led the way out across the stage. The curtains were closed. Stella could hear the orchestra playing and the rumble of many voices. On the stage, people were milling around, pulling on ropes and shouting instructions. A backdrop was being lowered, with a picture of a romantic-looking ruined castle, a stormy sky, a shipwreck, and a lighthouse.

The enormous mechanical sea monster waited at the side of the stage. A man on a ladder adjusted something inside its open mouth, called out "All right, Ned," and pulled his head out of the way. There was a click and a hiss and the sea monster belched out a flickering tongue of orange flame.

Stella jumped.

On the far side of the stage was another group of dancers, dressed as sailors with jaunty little blue-and-white caps.

"Mr. Capelli!" The boy was pushing his way through the people. "Mr. Capelli, sir. The Professor wants you."

The Professor was making his way quickly toward them. Mr. Capelli stepped in front of Stella, shielding her from view. "Hide!" he whispered.

She ducked behind the dancers, heart thumping.

Mr. Capelli said in a low voice, his eyes on the Professor, "I will keep him busy. The stage door is just along there." He flapped a hand. "Good-bye and good luck, Stella Montgomery."

"Good-bye, Mr. Capelli. Thank you," she whispered to his back. She crept along behind the dancers in the direction he had indicated.

She looked back for a moment. The Professor had reached Mr. Capelli and was bending toward him. Alfredo arched his back angrily, his tail like a bottle brush.

Stella saw the sign, STAGE DOOR. She hurried toward it. A doorman in uniform stood talking to a woman who held a number of hoops and three puffy white poodles.

The door opened suddenly and four or five girls, not much bigger than Stella, tumbled in, panting and laughing.

The daylight was bright after the gloom of the theater. Stella blinked. Outside, on the pier, flags fluttered, the merry-go-round turned, and the steam organ played a cheerful wheezing tune.

Families strolled by, wrapped up in coats and shawls. Boys shouted, their boots thumping on the boards of the pier. In the distance, Stella could see the Hotel Majestic, perched like a fancy hat on the cliff above Withering-by-Sea.

She had almost reached the door when it was pushed wide again and a man with pale whiskers, a furtive expression, and an amaranth waistcoat with a pattern of gardenias elbowed his way in.

It was the kidnapper, Scuttler, and he was dragging Ben behind him.

Eighteen

Stella gasped. Scuttler pushed his way into the theater through the stage door, gripping Ben by the arm and pulling him roughly along. Poor Ben was pale and his eyes were red from crying.

Before Scuttler could see her, Stella turned and darted back toward the stage. Behind, she heard him call out, "Professor! Professor! I found the boy."

She searched for Mr. Capelli in the groups of performers clustered in the wings, but she could not see him. Then she glimpsed the Professor. Limelight glinted on the lenses of his spectacles as he stalked through the crowd toward Scuttler and Ben. He would pass right by her. She looked around desperately for somewhere to hide.

A bell rang and a man said, "Silence. Silence there."

The trumpets played a fanfare and the audience applauded.

The show was starting.

The mermaids and sailors danced out onto the stage. Bright limelight sparkled on their costumes.

> *"Oh! 'Twas on the deep Atlantic in the*
> *equinoctial gales,*
> *That a sailor lad fell overboard among the*
> *sharks and whales."*

Stella clutched the Atlas to her chest, shrank back against the wall into shadow, and held her breath. The Professor had not seen her yet, but he would, any moment.

The girls who had dashed in through the stage door had been seized by a large woman. She scolded them in a whisper and hurried them through the crowd. As they passed Stella, the woman hissed, "I'll learn you to be late again," and slapped at their heads.

Stella took a breath and squeezed in amongst the girls just as the Professor strode past. He didn't look in her direction. She was swept away from him. The Professor reached Scuttler and Ben and spoke in a low, angry voice.

"Where did you find him?"

"Railway station." Scuttler gave Ben a vicious shake. "Trying to sneak on a train."

Ben cringed away from the Professor, his face white. He struggled to escape from Scuttler's grip.

Stella tried to look over her shoulder, to see what the Professor was doing to Ben, but the large woman slapped her on the back of her head. "Move."

She was pushed along with the other girls. None of them noticed her. The large woman hurried them upstairs, along a passage, around a corner, and into a small, extremely cluttered dressing room. She snapped, "Quick as you can, girls," and shut the door.

Clotheslines were strung from wall to wall, hung with stockings and underwear. The girls ducked underneath, flinging off their hats and coats and unwrapping their scarves. The room was already crowded with girls, chattering and giggling. Some were changing into dancing shoes and short, sequined dresses of pink and yellow and white. Some were

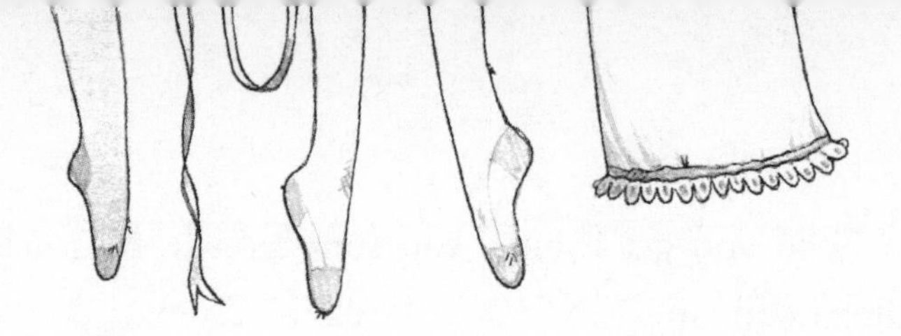

brushing out their hair and curling ringlets around their fingers.

Stella tucked herself into a dark corner, behind the door, half-hidden by coats hanging on pegs. It was dusty and her throat tickled. She held her breath and hoped she would have a chance to sneak away, unnoticed.

She needed to escape from the theater, but the Professor's men were everywhere. She was too conspicuous, wearing her dressing gown and slippers. A page from the Atlas came into her mind: a map of Mexico and California. In the margin, the tiny figure of a man wearing antlers on his head crept through a herd of deer in a thick forest. *The hunter dons a cunning disguise and arms himself with arrows tipped with rattlesnake venom.*

She needed a cunning disguise. The theater was full of costumes and clothes of all kinds. It should be easy to find something.

"You're late, Gert," said one of the girls.

"Mrs. MacTaggerty caught us coming in. She's in a right tizz," said a tallish girl with a cheerful face covered in freckles. She turned her back to a ginger-haired girl. "Unbutton me, Annie."

"Did you get them?" someone asked. "Mrs. Mac didn't cop 'em?"

The freckled girl rummaged in the coat she had flung aside. She took a bulging paper bag of sweets from the pocket. "Bull's-eyes and Gibraltar rock and Curly Andrews and apple gundy," she announced.

The girls whooped and squealed and scrambled forward. Gert held the bag out to a small, dark-haired girl who had already changed into her costume. "Pass 'em round, Ettie," she said, and took her dress off over her head. She pulled off her stockings and felt along the clothesline for a dry pair. She pushed some aside, and her gaze slid across Stella without noticing her. Stella shut her eyes and tried to sink into the shadow. But the dust caught in her nose and she suddenly sneezed.

Gert gave a start. "Nobble me Granny!"

The other girls turned to look.

"Who's that?" someone asked.

"Why's she skrivin' there?"

"Who're you?" asked Gert.

She didn't look unfriendly. Stella gave her a nervous smile.

"I'm—" she started to say.

"I reckon she's that kid the Professor's after," said

Annie indistinctly, her mouth full of toffee. "Professor says she stole something."

"That right?" Gert asked Stella.

Stella shook her head. "No, I never stole anything. I'm not a thief. Please don't tell him I'm here."

Gert grinned. "We won't tell him. Will we, girls?"

The other girls made agreeing noises.

"He's horrible. He's right mean to that boy he's got."

"He gives me the frights."

"Me too."

"He don't frighten me," said Gert.

"Nobody frightens Gert," said Annie, giggling.

"She put a dirty great oyster in his coat pocket."

"And cockles in his slippers."

"And that dead jellyfish in his top hat."

They all laughed.

"Have one." Ettie offered Stella the bag. Stella looked inside. The sweets were vivid colors: green, red, yellow, and black. Some looked like tiny striped satin cushions, some like shards of broken glass, and some like round, gleaming jewels. Stella hesitated. Aunt Deliverance said sweets were both vulgar and unwholesome.

"Go on," said Ettie with a grin.

Stella took one. It was a glossy red with a swirl

of white, like the pattern of a snail shell. It tasted of treacle and peppermint. It was delicious.

"We got a tip from an old gent," said Gert, popping a lurid green sweet into her mouth and lacing up her dancing shoes. "A florin. And so we sneaked out and got 'em. While Mrs. Mac's back was turned." She stood, pointed her toes, and kicked high with one leg and then the other. "I'm Gert," she said, and held out her hand to Stella.

Stella pushed the sweet into her cheek with her tongue and said, 'I'm Stella.' They shook hands.

Gert pointed to the girls, one by one. "This is Ettie, Annie, Lizzie, Mary, another Mary, Maggie, Edna, another Mary, Bess, Hattie, and that's little Elsie."

"Are you dancers?" asked Stella.

"We're the Fairy Bells," said Gert, grinning. "We do fancy dancing, kicks, flip-flaps and that." She took a yellow dress off a peg, shook it out, and pulled it over her head. "Button me up."

Stella put the Atlas under her arm and did the best she could with the long row of tiny buttons. It was difficult, because Gert kept jiggling and doing complicated, clever dance steps. "There," Stella said at last.

"Ta." Gert spun on her toes.

Stella said, "Do you earn money as dancers?"

"Of course. But only half a crown and keep in the winter. And Mrs. Mac makes us put a penny in the plate on Sundays. And with stockings a tanner a pair, I can only send one and six to my granny each week. There are five little ones at home with her, and only me earning. It ain't so tough in the summer; then we go all along the coast, and there's four or five shows a day."

"Don't you do lessons?" asked Stella enviously.

"'Course not. We're all finished with school. Even little Elsie's ten, and some of us are thirteen." Gert fluffed out her ringlets and grinned. "Why's the Professor after you, girl? He's saying you nicked something."

"He says I did, but I didn't. I need to get out of the theater. I think I need a disguise," said Stella. "A cunning disguise. So he won't recognize me."

Gert assessed Stella with her head to the side. "She's about the size of some of them imps, ain't she, Annie? We could dress her up like a boy and sneak her out the stage door."

Annie pushed her way through the girls and looked Stella up and down. "I reckon."

"We could shove her hair up in a cap," said Ettie.

"Nip along, Annie," said Gert. "Get some old clothes from them boys." She turned to Stella as

Annie left. "Her little brother's one of the imps in the big musical number. There's ten of them what pull the fairy queen's carriage."

The girls surrounded Stella and pulled off her dressing gown.

"Put that book down for a jiffy," said Gert.

"This is a good dressing gown," said Ettie. "Good quality."

"And cop this lace." One of the girls ran her fingers along the hem of Stella's nightgown.

Stella was in her vest and drawers by the time Annie hurried back into the room with an armful of clothes.

"What's that?" asked Ettie, pointing at Mr. Filbert's package.

"Nothing," said Stella quickly. She pushed the little pocket down under her vest.

Gert rummaged through the clothes and held out a shirt and a pair of trousers. Stella pulled them on. The shirt was enormous; it hung down to her knees and flapped beyond her hands. The girls tucked it in and rolled up the sleeves.

"Here," said Gert. She tied a piece of string around the waist of the trousers.

There was a short blue felt coat with buttoned pockets and many darns and patches. The sleeves were too long, so Gert folded over the cuffs several times. The girls coiled Stella's hair up on top of her head, thrust in several pins, and then crammed a felt cap over it. They all giggled.

"Try these old boots," said Annie. Stella pushed her bare feet into them, and someone laced them up. They were thick leather with nails in the soles.

"Look!" Many hands pushed her across the room to the washstand, where a broken mirror leaned against the wall.

She looked into the mirror, and a strange boy looked back at her. He had a pale face and round eyes. She gave him a smile, and he smiled back nervously. She did not recognize herself at all. Stella said awkwardly, "I'm sorry, I haven't money for the clothes."

"That's all right," said Gert. "Those boys won't miss 'em."

"Are you sure? I mean, why don't you take the dressing gown and the nightgown and the slippers?" suggested Stella tentatively. The Aunts would be angry, but she had nothing else to offer.

"Well, that's bang-up," said Gert with a grin. She held out her hand and Stella shook it. "Come on then, I'll show you the way." She opened the door, peeped out, and beckoned Stella to follow.

Stella picked up the Atlas and waved at the girls. "Good-bye," she said. "Thank you."

The girls called, "Good-bye. Good luck!"

Stella waved again and followed Gert from the room.

Nineteen

Gert led Stella along a passage. Stella's feet felt clumsy in the clomping nailed boots, and the trousers made her legs feel as if they belonged to someone else.

One of the Professor's men came out of a doorway. Stella lowered her head, heart thumping, but he hardly glanced at them as they passed. Her cunning disguise was working.

"Stage door's this way." Gert led her down a narrow flight of stairs.

Halfway down, Stella gasped and clutched Gert's arm. They froze.

Just below, at the bottom of the stairs, the Professor, Scuttler, and Ben stood in shadow. Scuttler gripped Ben by the shoulder. The Professor felt in his pocket with his long, pale fingers and pulled out the bottle of ink. He reached a hand out toward Ben. The ring on his finger glinted red.

Ben was crying. He struggled and said, "No, no. I won't do it. I won't say nothing."

"Quick. This way," whispered Gert. She grabbed Stella's hand and pulled her away, back up the stairs. "Come on." She led the way back along the passageway, around a corner, and down another flight of stairs, ducking under hanging ropes and pulleys, and then crept along a short, dark passage beside the stage.

They came to a narrow door. Beyond, the orchestra was playing and Stella could hear the audience laughing and applauding. Gert put her finger to her lips and whispered, "This is the pass door." She pulled the bolt and opened the door a crack. "Here you go," she said.

Stella peeped through the crack. Gaslight glittered on marble columns and mirrors and gilt cherubs. The door was to the side of the stage, in a dark corner, close to the front rows of the audience. Hundreds of faces were watching the stage. The music was loud and close. People were calling out, hooting and applauding.

"There's the main door," said Gert, pointing. "Straight out back there. You can get out that way."

Stella hesitated. Gert gave her a little push. "Go

on, then, girl," she said. "I've got to get back. We're on any minute."

Stella swallowed and slipped through the door. "Thank you," she whispered.

"Good luck," said Gert with a grin, and closed the door.

The air was thick with tobacco smoke and smelled of oranges and burnt toffee. Lights glittered and sparkled. Nobody seemed to notice Stella. Everyone was watching the stage, where limelight shone on a lady dressed in pink feathers, circling on a high-wheeled bicycle. The orchestra was playing a waltz, and the bicycling lady was singing in a trilling voice,

"Wheeling along with the greatest of speed,
That dashing young girl on her velocipede."

Stella crept up the aisle at the side of the audience. Nutshells crunched under her feet. A man with a tray of kidney pies pushed past. "Watch it, lad," he said.

At the back of the theater was a row of glass doors, and beyond them Stella could see the marble foyer and daylight. The way out. She had almost reached the doors when they swung open and several large men shouldered their way into the theater. She gasped. At any moment they would see her. She was trapped. She darted back down the aisle, spied an empty seat, and slipped into it.

It was at the end of a row, beside a large family. There were two plump boys in Norfolk suits, eating toffee. Beside them sat the mother, with a fat baby on her lap. Beyond her was the father, wearing a purple waistcoat, and several little girls in frilled dresses. Orange peel and toffee papers were scattered all around them. None of them paid Stella any attention.

She swallowed.

On the stage, the bicycling lady dismounted, curtsied several times, blew a kiss, and ran from the stage. A man stepped out and announced, "And now, for your pleasure, ladies and gentlemen. The renowned Mr. Portendo, Basso Profundo."

Stella risked a glance around. Perhaps the men would not recognize her, dressed as a boy. There were many boys in the audience. Could she creep out, hidden in the crowd, at the end of the show? That would be the safest way to escape. Unless Ben had already told the Professor where she was.

If they tried to grab her, she would scream.

A boy came down the aisle with a tray of ginger beer bottles, and then a girl with a basket of oranges.

The violins played a swirling, rising melody, and an enormous man with glossy black whiskers strode out in front of the curtain. He sang a sad song about being away from his love. His voice was like a foghorn.

There were sniffles throughout the audience. The mother of the large family wiped her eyes with her handkerchief, and the father blew his nose, making a sound like a trumpet.

Stella darted another glance behind. The men were looming, dark shapes at the back of the theater. She sank down in her seat, her heart thumping.

The enormous man sang a second sad song and then bowed deeply and left the stage as the audience sobbed and clapped.

The announcer called, "And now, ladies and gentlemen. The charming Fairy Bells."

The orchestra played a polka, and the twelve Fairy Bells skipped onto the stage, smiling and sparkling in the limelight. They whirled around, turning this way and that in time to the music. They linked arms and kicked their legs high. They jumped and leaped. One girl (Ettie, Stella thought) flipped over onto her hands and back onto her feet, and the others followed, twirling over and over. Stella could hardly believe they were the same girls she had met in their dressing room, giggling and eating sweets. They were so clever, they seemed as if they were from another world.

The dance ended and the audience cheered. The Fairy Bells stood in a row on the stage, curtsied, and ran off.

The announcer stepped out again. "Ladies and gentlemen, the Extraordinary Conjurer and Magician, Professor Starke."

There was a moment of silence and then a drumroll. The gaslights in the theater dimmed and the lights on the stage went out. A murmur went around the audience.

The curtains drew apart and a figure appeared on the darkened stage. The Professor was dressed in black and wore a tall hat. His eyes were hidden behind the green, glinting lenses of his spectacles.

He waved his hand, cymbals clashed, and dozens of candles flared into light on three tall candelabra. The audience gasped.

"Welcome, ladies and gentlemen," said the Professor, and reached out with a flourish. A large bunch of white flowers appeared in his hand out of nowhere. He twirled the flowers and flung them into the air. As they scattered, they turned into a flock of screeching bats and flapped away into the darkness.

"Venture into the unknown to witness marvels

of magic." The Professor strode across the stage to a glass bowl full of water resting on top of a pillar. He took a gold coin from his pocket and tapped it against the bowl. It made a clear ringing sound. He tossed the coin into the water. It changed into a fat goldfish and swam around the bowl.

He plunged his hand in, caught the fish, and lifted it out of the water. The little fish glinted in the candlelight and then, with a flash, it burst into flames. The audience gasped. Fire engulfed the Professor's hand. The golden flames flickered and blazed, and then dwindled and died away. Between his blackened, smoking fingers was a gleaming golden coin. He twirled it, and dropped it back into his pocket and bowed. The crowd applauded.

He turned to a tall box in the center of the stage. It was glossy black with a pattern of gold stars. It was the size of a narrow wardrobe. The Professor opened the door and showed the interior to the audience. It was empty.

He said, "Ladies and gentlemen. Allow me to demonstrate the Cabinet of Mysteries."

There was another drumroll. Stella looked quickly behind her. Something was happening at the back of the theater, some kind of disturbance, raised voices and scuffling.

Onstage, the Professor removed his hat, reached inside, and pulled out a large gray rabbit. He placed the rabbit on the floor of the cabinet and shut the door. There was a clash of cymbals and a loud bang. Smoke billowed. The Professor waved his long fingers and flung open the door of the cabinet. The rabbit was gone. In its place was a small pile of blackened bones and a scattering of ashes. There were shrieks in the audience.

He held out his hands. "And now I need a brave volunteer. Who will be courageous and step into the Cabinet of Mysteries?"

The gaslights in the auditorium flared up again.

Children pushed and shoved one another and squealed and craned their necks around. People hooted and whistled. But nobody stood up.

"Come, ladies and gentlemen. Venture onto the stage and step into the unknown," said the Professor.

Suddenly a figure appeared beside Stella. It was Scuttler. Before she could think, he clasped her wrist and pulled her to her feet.

"Professor. Here's a volunteer," he called.

Stella's heart lurched. She could hardly breathe. "No, no," she gasped.

"Come up onstage, my boy," said the Professor with a thin smile.

The audience cheered. Scuttler dragged Stella down the aisle to the stage. She tried to twist her hand away, but his grip tightened and she yelped in pain.

He pulled her up a narrow flight of stairs. She dropped the Atlas. Before she could pick it up, Scuttler jerked her away roughly and dragged her onto the stage. "Hold still, brat," he muttered, "or you'll get hurt."

The Professor said, "Welcome our brave volunteer." He gestured at Stella. The audience clapped and hooted and whistled, and the orchestra played. The lights were dazzling. Stella looked out at rows and rows of grinning, shouting faces. The noise was like waves crashing on shingle.

She looked around desperately. The Professor's men stood all around the edges of the stage. There was no escape. She saw Ben in the shadows, pale and miserable, his hands black with ink.

"Now, my boy, step into the Cabinet of Mysteries," said the Professor.

Scuttler dragged Stella across to the cabinet and pushed her inside. The Professor slammed the door.

She was trapped.

She flung herself against the door, but it was shut tight. She yelled and thrashed and kicked. The music from the orchestra and the roars from the audience were deafening.

There was a clash of cymbals, a loud bang, and choking smoke. The floor dropped away under her and she tumbled down into darkness.

Twenty

Stella landed hard, the breath knocked out of her. Rough hands grabbed her. She kicked and struggled. Her flailing boot connected with something soft. A man cursed. Her head hit something. She was pinned to the ground. An evil-smelling cloth was shoved into her mouth and she was bundled up into a blanket. She could not move; she could barely breathe.

There was a scuffle somewhere nearby, a confused jumble of voices.

"Stop! Police! Help!"

"Grab that one too. Don't let her scarper."

"Let go!"

There was a yell, more scuffling, and a man cursed again. "She bleedin' bit me."

The world spun around.

Stella woke and slept and woke again as she was jolted uncomfortably. Her head hurt. It was dark. She struggled but could not move. There were voices nearby. She tried to call out but could not make any sound. She was dizzy and felt as if she might be sick.

❧

She woke again and her head felt a bit clearer. She was lying on something hard. There was a lurching motion, creaking, and horses' hooves and the rumbling sound of cart wheels. She tried to move, but her arms and legs were pinned. Things were piled on top of her. Was it day or night? She felt as if she might choke. Her mouth was full of cloth. It tasted revolting, of sweat and tobacco. She managed to spit it out and gasped for air. The hairy blanket covered her head, rough against her cheek. She wriggled around and tried to turn over, but she could not move. Her head hurt. She slept again.

❧

Time passed. The cart was slowing. Someone called to the horse, the harness jingled, and the cart came to a halt. Men's voices spoke, above her and close-by.

"Here's the causeway, Charlie."

"It's right creepy out here."

"Take a nip of this. It'll put heart in you." Stella heard the chink of a bottle.

One of the men gasped. "Look."

"What?"

"There, Scuttler. Just there. I seen another one."

"Bleedin' fiddle-faddle. There ain't nothing."

"My gran told me about them lights," said Charlie, his voice low and quavering. "They lead you out into the marsh and nab the soul right out of your chest."

"There ain't no such thing," said Scuttler. "Your gran was off with the fairies. Take another nip."

Charlie said, "Sun's nearly gone down."

"Sooner we get over, sooner we get back."

There was a distant sobbing cry. As it died away, Charlie muttered, "Cripes. This place gives me the shivers."

"Me too, Charlie. Me too. But think on this. There ain't no police on our tail. We got the nippers away, and we got away clear. They're still watching the theater, likely. Watching the Professor. Ha-ha. They never looked in the laundry basket." He laughed. "It's a golden strike for me and you, Charlie. And off to the Smoke for us."

"What'll happen to the nippers?" asked Charlie.

"Not our affair," said Scuttler firmly. "Don't you go soft on me now. This time tomorrow, we'll be far away." He chirruped to the horse, and the cart started moving again.

Where were they going? Desperately Stella struggled to move, but it felt as if bundles of clothes were piled on top of her, weighing her down.

Close by her ear, someone groaned, making her jump. Who else had they captured?

"Is anyone there?" Stella tried to whisper, but her throat was dry, and the blanket muffled the sound. There was no answer.

She twisted her head from side to side, trying to free it from the enveloping blanket. She wriggled determinedly until she uncovered one eye. Her face was pressed against the wall of a basket. She blinked and peered out between the gaps in the wicker.

She had a lurching, flickering view of the world outside. She was in a basket on the back of a cart. She could see a narrow road winding away behind. The land was flat and marshy, with scattered rocky outcrops and stunted, twisted trees. The last of the daylight reflected on pools of stagnant water. It was gray and misty and raining.

She could smell salt and dead fish. The cart jolted across sand and seaweed. Stella could hear waves breaking on shingle. Then, all at once, they were traveling on a causeway, out over the sea.

The causeway was only a few inches clear of the water. The flagstones were uneven and broken, and draped with seaweed. The cart rocked. What if it overturned? Dark water stretched away on both sides and lapped at the edges of the causeway. It looked deep and cold. Stella was trapped in the basket and she could not move. She did not want to drown. Her heart thudded as she watched the shoreline until it dwindled and became only a vague gray blur in the rain. Then it was lost behind, and she could see only the narrow causeway stretching across the gray water, and the darkening sky above. She shivered.

"Tide's coming in," said Charlie, sounding nervous.

A wave broke over the causeway, the foam like lace.

"Sooner we get there, sooner we get back." Scuttler clicked his tongue to the horse. The harness jingled and the cart gave a frightening lurch.

An uneven line of poles marked the edge of the causeway. A black bird with a long neck was perched on top of a pole, a wriggling silver fish in its beak. As the cart trundled past, the bird swallowed the fish, made a loud cry, and flapped away.

Another wave broke over the causeway with a rush. Stiff with fear, Stella watched the dark water swirling around the wheels of the cart. Minutes passed. At last the cart began to climb up and away from the sea, past rocks and scrubby plants.

Stella hadn't realized she had been holding her breath. She let it out with a shuddering gasp.

The cart stopped. The men jumped down. The basket jerked and then the lid opened and things were lifted off her. She was pulled and dragged and then slung over a shoulder and carried.

She had a glimpse of a jumble of rocks, and stone steps leading up to a tall tower. It had an uneven, broken outline against the sky. As if it had been once part of something larger. A castle, perhaps. She could see water all around. An island.

A key turned in a lock, and then she was carried up a narrow spiral staircase. Up and up. Another door opened and she was dumped down onto a hard floor.

It was a small round room. Broken furniture and a torn tapestry lay in a heap. A tiny window with no glass let in the rain. Stella struggled to free herself from the entangling blanket. She was shaking and numb with cold.

Charlie came in and dropped another bundle onto the floor.

"Gert!" gasped Stella. Gert had a piece of dirty cloth fixed around her mouth and was wrapped in sacking and tied with rope. She was making muffled, angry noises, and her eyes looked furious.

Scuttler glared at Gert. "She was yelling for the coppers, so we had to nab her too. Serves her right. Spitfire." He rubbed a painful-looking red mark on his wrist. He turned to Stella. "You've given us a mort of trouble, girl. The Professor's in a right fury. Turning the boy against him. And now all them police crawlin' everywhere, watching him. Suspicious. Take you right away out here, he says. Sort this out for good. Where you can't give no more trouble."

Stella bit her lip so she would not cry.

"Professor'll be here next low tide," said Scuttler as they turned to leave. "You give him his thingabob and all's rug. Think on that."

"Please don't leave us here," said Stella, shivering.

"Tide's coming in, Scuttler," said Charlie, halfway out the door.

"Think on that." Scuttler turned back, his face close to Stella's. His furtive eyes were pale and milky, like undercooked eggs. His breath smelled of gin and old meat. "Give the Professor his little niggle thing, and you and your friend, both of you, are back home safe, like nothing happened. Otherwise . . ." He shrugged and, without more words, turned and left, slamming and locking the heavy door behind him.

Otherwise . . . Stella heard the men's footsteps hurrying away down the stairs. She crawled across to Gert and pulled off her gag. She tried to untie the rope. Her fingers were cold and stiff, and she had to use her teeth to loosen the knots.

Below, a door slammed.

Gert spluttered and coughed. She said, "Flipping heck," and spat bits of cloth out of her mouth. "Nobble me Granny. Stinking gumbleguts. Mangle their gizzards. I bit one of 'em, though. Made him flipping yell." She gave a satisfied grin. She pulled away the rope and sacking and stretched her arms and legs. She was still wearing her spangled yellow dancing dress. She rubbed her arms and did some jiggling dance steps. "Cripes, it's freezing. Where are we? Can we get out?"

"I don't know." Stella stood up stiffly, stumbled across the room, and clambered onto a broken chair to look out of the narrow window. A gust of icy wind and a spatter of raindrops blew in. She leaned on the sill and looked down. Far below, in the fading light, the causeway stretched away across the sea. Parts of it were already underwater. The cart drove back along it. Waves lapped around its wheels.

Gert climbed up beside her, and together they watched the cart until it dwindled to a tiny dark shape and was lost in the dusk and the rain.

"Blimey," said Gert.

Stella climbed down and went to the door. She rattled the rusty iron handle back and forth uselessly. She looked around the tiny room and shivered again. It was cold, and getting colder. It would soon be dark. The heavy door was locked. The window was too narrow to climb through, and too high up. There was no other way to escape.

They were trapped, quite alone, in the middle of the sea.

Twenty-One

High up in the tower, Stella and Gert huddled together, wrapped in the torn tapestry, the sacking, and the blanket. The tapestry was damp and stiff and smelled of mold, but it was thick and kept out some of the cold. Outside, the wind howled. Swirling gusts of icy air blew in through the window. Stella shivered.

"I knew the Professor was a twisty cove, all along," Gert said. "I saw him shove you in his cabinet. I know how that trick works. It's simple. There's a trapdoor, it opens under, and drops down, like that. So I ran down under the stage to save you. But them skitching rumguzzlers caught me, too."

"I'm sorry," said Stella.

"Weren't your fault." Gert shrugged. "I should've gone straight for the coppers. They were everywhere, looking for you. I didn't stop and think. Mrs. Mac's always saying, 'Think first, girl.' She'll be throwing fifty fits right now. D'you reckon the police'll be able to find us, all the way out here?"

Stella said, "I hope so." But it seemed unlikely. How would they know where to look?

"So what'll we do when the Professor gets here? I'll flipping bite him, too. I'll make him yell."

"We should run," said Stella. "He can't catch both of us. Perhaps one of us can get away from him and run along the causeway to get help, if the tide's out."

"I'll bite him first. Then I'll run," said Gert. "What's he after, anyway?"

"He wants this little thing." Stella put a hand to her chest, where Mr. Filbert's package was hidden.

"What thing? What is it?" asked Gert.

"I don't know," said Stella. She pulled out the pocket and unwrapped the little silver bottle. "Look."

Gert took it gingerly. She turned it over in her hands, and it gleamed in the darkness. Out of the corner of her eye, Stella had a glimpse of something silvery flickering. She turned quickly but saw nothing but shadows.

"There's something inside," Gert said, peering into the bottle. "I saw it move." She shuddered. "That's right creepy. What's in there?"

"I don't know," said Stella again. "Ben was telling me, but he didn't finish the story. It was about a sorcerer from the olden days. The Grimpen Sorcerer. I think the bottle belonged to him."

"Is Ben that boy the Professor's got?" asked Gert. Without waiting for an answer, she went on, "When there's a big storm, my granny says the Grimpen Serpent's swimming again. But that's just an old saying."

"Ben said the Grimpen Sorcerer could change into a serpent," said Stella, remembering.

Gert shrugged. "Sounds like a fairy story to me." She handed the bottle back to Stella. "Well, it gives me the frights," she said.

"I wish I knew what to do with it." Stella wrapped it up and tucked it away.

"It's something bad, isn't it? We can't let the Professor get it. He's up to no good, he is. Perhaps you should chuck it in the sea," suggested Gert, eyeing the window. "Get rid of it."

"No, I promised to keep it safe," said Stella. "I promised Mr. Filbert, and he's dead now. The Professor stabbed him."

"Dead!" gasped Gert. "Cripes." She thought for a second. "Well, then sniggle it away somewhere and come back for it later."

Stella shook her head. "No. The best chance would be to run, if we can. I can't hide it. Ben can see things that have happened. The Professor makes him look into a pool of ink, and he sees things there. If I hid it somewhere, Ben would see, and he'll tell the Professor."

"I thought that boy was like that,' said Gert. 'You know. Uncanny."

"Fey?" asked Stella.

"Some people say that. Off with the fairies. We had a girl dancing in the Fairy Bells once. Tottie. She was like that. She was always listening to something nobody else could hear. She said it was the fairies singing. But Mrs. Mac wouldn't have it. She locked Tottie in the cupboard until she stopped talking about it."

"But why?"

"Well, it ain't respectable, is it? Mrs. Mac's right proper. 'Elbows off the flippin' table, girls. Don't chew with your gobs open,'" Gert said in a prim voice, and giggled. "Respectable people don't talk about that havey-cavey stuff. And if they've got something like that in their family, they keep it quiet. They don't want people to know their great-great-grandpa was part mermaid or sorcerer or fairy, or something. Or turned into a dirty big pumpkin at midnight, like in the old stories. Or used to lurk about under bridges and then jump out and eat people." She snorted with laughter.

Stella remembered Aunt Temperance saying, *We never speak of such things. Never.* There was nobody more respectable than the Aunts. No wonder they would not answer her questions.

After a moment she said, "Ben thought I might be fey. But I can't do anything like that. I can't see things that have happened, like Ben, and I can't hear fairies singing."

Gert shrugged. "Perhaps it's something else with you."

Stella shivered. Ben had said exactly the same thing. She imagined something hiding inside her chest. Something dark and secret. Like the thing that lurked inside Mr. Filbert's bottle. She swallowed. "But I'm not like that," she said. "I'm just ordinary."

Gert shrugged again and pulled the tapestry more tightly around their shoulders. "It runs in families, that kind of thing," she said. "Anyone in your family a bit peculiar?"

"I live with my Aunts. They're peculiar, but they're very respectable. My parents died when I was little. I don't know anything about them."

"My mam's dead too, and my dad's gone," said Gert. "I've got five little brothers. Little monkeys, the lot of 'em. They live with our granny. You got brothers or sisters?"

"No, there's only me," said Stella. But she remembered the photograph she had found in Aunt Temperance's album. "At least, I think there's only me," she said.

"Don't you know?"

Stella explained about the photograph. "In the picture, there was a lady and two babies. It said '*P, S* and *L*' on the back. My mother was called Patience, so perhaps it's a picture of her. *P* for Patience and *S* for Stella. I don't know about *L*. Maybe I had a sister, do you think? But now I've lost the photograph. It was in my Atlas, and I dropped it at the theater. It's gone. And my Aunts never answer my questions.

I want to try to find out. But I don't know how."

"Don't say 'I'll try,' girl. Say 'I will,'" said Gert firmly. "That's what Mrs. Mac says. It's like when I was little, and she was learning me handsprings. If you think you can't do it, you hesitate, and you land smack on your face. You have to say to yourself, 'I can do this,' and believe it."

Gert seemed very sure of herself. Stella wished she could feel so confident. "I will find out," she said, as definitely as she could manage.

"Mind you, it takes practice to do a handspring," said Gert. "You land smack on your face anyway, a whole lot of times."

"I'll find out somehow," said Stella.

"Family's important," said Gert. "You got to know who you are."

Later Stella dreamed of dark water rising. Rippling, as if something were swimming just below the surface. Rising higher and higher. Swirling around her legs, pulling her off-balance. Lapping at her chest, rising higher, over her head. She couldn't breathe. Her mouth was full of water. There was no air. Something was howling.

She woke suddenly, gasping for breath. She stared

into darkness. The wind sounded like voices crying.

Without thinking, she groped for the Atlas. But then she remembered it was lost. A sob caught in her throat. It had been trampled underfoot at the theater and swept up with the rubbish. Even in the darkness, she could have stroked its cover and thought of the comforting pictures inside. Fighting her rising panic, she tried to remember something encouraging from the Atlas. She knew it by heart.

But it was difficult to remember properly. She was too frightened. She remembered only a jumble of things.

A picture of a tall ship caught in sea ice, torn apart and drifting.

Another picture of a dark, stormy sea, crashing waves, and jagged lightning; a high, whirling waterspout threatening a small fishing boat.

A picture of a terrified horse, eyes rolling, splashing and struggling knee-deep in a river, attacked by an enormous snakelike fish. *The gymnotus, or electric eel, can kill the largest animal, when in full galvanic vigor.*

She shuddered, curled up tightly beside Gert, pulled the tapestry over her head, stuffed her fingers in her ears, and shut her eyes.

The wind wailed. Every creak in the tower made

her stiffen in fright. She thought of her bedroom at the hotel, familiar and safe, with the Aunts snoring in the next room. She wished she were back home.

She cried until she was exhausted, and at last fell asleep.

A loud bang woke Stella and she sat up, heart thumping. She strained her ears but could hear nothing but the wind and the sea.

She felt for Gert and shook her shoulder. 'Wake up,' she whispered.

"What?" mumbled Gert, sitting up.

Stella clutched her arm. "I heard something."

A moment passed, and then they heard voices, another bang, and footsteps coming up the stairs. Stella held her breath. She could feel Gert trembling.

A light flickered under the door, a key rattled in the lock, and the door opened. The lantern light was dazzling.

A figure stood in the doorway, gaunt and dark, his tall hat and long coat streaming with water.

It was the Professor.

Twenty-Two

The Professor took two strides into the room. Light reflected on the lenses of his spectacles. Stella swallowed. She tried to say something but only managed to make a croaking noise. The Professor reached down and took hold of her arm and dragged her to her feet. Stella tried to pull away, but she was shaking and stiff with cold, and his grip was too strong. He reached down again and seized Gert. She twisted in his grasp, clawing at his gloved hand with her fingernails.

"Let go," she gasped.

The Professor ignored their struggles, dragged them to the door, and pushed them ahead of him down the steep, winding stairs. Stella stumbled and nearly fell.

At the bottom of the stairs was a wide hallway.

Flurries of cold rain blew in through an archway from the darkness outside. The Professor pulled them along the hallway, toward a small door. It stood ajar, and a dim light shone from the room beyond.

Gert twisted around suddenly and shoved the Professor off-balance. He dropped the lantern. It shattered on the stone floor.

In the darkness, Stella yelled, "Gert, run!" She grabbed the Professor's arm and clung on. His coat was slippery and wet. "Run!" she shouted again.

Gert hesitated for a second and then turned and darted away through the archway and out into the storm. The Professor cursed. He shoved Stella to the floor, spun on his heel, and followed Gert, his long coat flapping behind him. Stella got to her feet and dashed after them.

Outside, icy rain pelted down. She could see flickering glimmers of foam on the crashing waves below. Stone steps led down toward the causeway.

She started to climb down. The steps were uneven and slippery. She could only go slowly, one step at a time. Not far below, she heard sounds of a struggle. The Professor cursed. Gert cried out in pain. Stella hesitated, straining her eyes to see ahead.

The Professor suddenly loomed up out of the darkness, dragging Gert behind him.

"Flipping skitching scumbucket. Let go of me," gasped Gert, struggling.

Stella turned to run, but before she could move, the Professor grabbed her arm and twisted it behind her with a painful jerk. She almost fell, but he wrenched her to her feet and pushed her and Gert back up the stairs, into the tower. He dragged them along the hallway and through the small doorway, into a candlelit room. He shut the door and turned the key in the lock.

The room was quiet. The thick stone walls muffled the sounds of the storm. The Professor's breath was coming in angry hisses through his clenched teeth. He removed his hat and his wet coat and hung them up beside the door. Gert's nose was bleeding, and she held her arm awkwardly across her body, as if the Professor had hurt her shoulder.

"Are you all right?" whispered Stella.

Gert nodded. "I'm prime," she said, but she was very pale, and looked shaken.

The room was lined with shelves of books, boxes, and bundles of paper. The Professor strode across to a workbench. There, a book lay open, closely written in spidery sepia ink. Woodworking tools hung in neat rows, beside string and glue and jars of nails and pieces of wood. Tiny models of theater stages contained miniature wax figures performing magic tricks.

Mirrors everywhere reflected the flickering candlelight, but the high,

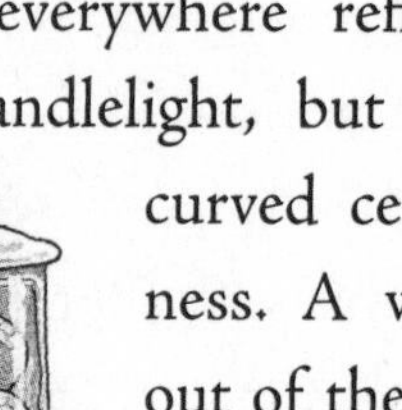

curved ceiling was lost in darkness. A wavering face appeared out of the shadows. Stella caught her breath but then saw it was her own reflection, so distorted and twisted by the curved surface of a mirror that she could barely recognize herself.

A pale snake was coiled in a jar of dark liquid. A strange little doll leered from a high shelf, beside a skull and a collection of blackened bones. A spindly insect was twisted and frozen inside a piece of amber.

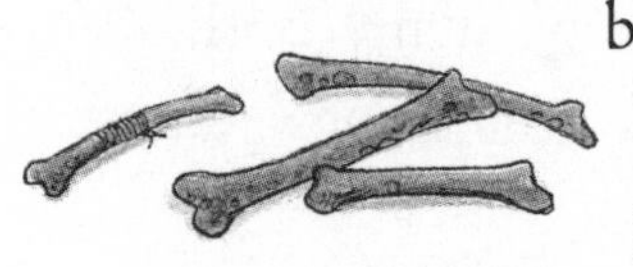

A movement caught Stella's eye. Ben was crouched by the fireplace, laying a fire.

The Professor took off his gloves. On his pale hand, the ring with the dark stone glimmered in the candlelight. He turned it on his finger and said, "Hurry, boy. Did you see to the horse?"

Ben looked up nervously, his eyes on the Professor's ring. He had a dark bruise on his cheek. He ducked his head and muttered, "Yes, sir," and turned back to the fire. He did not meet Stella's gaze.

"My workshop," said the Professor, with a flourish of his fingers. "This island is sufficiently secluded for my purposes. We magicians must guard our professional secrets. And I have many secrets. Some you have already encountered. Fortunately, you did not damage them beyond repair." He gestured to the workbench, and Stella saw the hand of glory, looking somewhat squashed. Beside it lay the little beetle with its legs in the air and its clockwork insides in a saucer.

"You have caused me much inconvenience." The Professor's voice was sharp. "You will regret your decision to concern yourself with my affairs. Both of you." He strode across the room. "It ends now. Give it to me."

"I don't have it," Stella said.

"You do."

Desperately, she backed away. Gert took a step toward him, but he pushed her aside easily and she collapsed against the wall with a moan of pain. He grasped Stella by the shoulders and shook her until her teeth rattled together and she was dizzy and close to tears.

He turned the ring on his finger. The dark stone glittered red in the candlelight. "Boy," he said, without taking his eyes from Stella. "Where is it?"

"No, Ben!" gasped Stella. "Don't tell him."

Ben's face was in shadow. In a low, miserable voice, as if the words were being pulled from his throat against his will, he said, "Around her neck."

"No!"

The Professor grasped her neck. Stella struggled, but he snaked his fingers under her shirt, found the ribbon, and pulled out Mr. Filbert's package. He snapped the ribbon with a sharp jerk and pushed her away. She stumbled backward and fell.

He closed his fingers over the little package. "At last," he murmured. "At last." He turned away from her and strode to his workbench. He took the package from the linen pocket and carefully unfolded the oilcloth and the paper.

"Consider yourselves fortunate," he said. "All of you. For what you are about to witness will be beyond anything you could imagine."

Stella swallowed and stammered, "D-don't." She pulled herself to her feet and took a shuddering breath. "Don't open it."

The Professor smiled. "You know nothing of this. In our modern age we have only distant echoes of the old powers. Diluted whispers that have passed down through the years, becoming weaker and weaker. Faint traces, in these pieces of gimcrack I have collected, and this boy and his feeble visions. Worthless tricks with mirrors and goldfish to impress an ignorant crowd. Memories of the marvels that once were." He turned the gleaming silver bottle in his long, pale fingers. There was a slithering noise. Shadows flickered across the walls. "But here, in this bottle, here is power. Sealed and hidden, untainted by the years that have passed."

Stella glanced at Ben. He was sitting hunched beside the fire, his ink-stained hands covering his face. Shadow, the kitten, was on his shoulder, watching the Professor, her fur spiky and her eyes huge and dark.

The Professor said, "Those who hid this thought it would be forgotten. That the hazel tree would keep it concealed forever. Fools try to hide what they cannot understand, what they fear. But I studied the books and untangled the mysteries and found where it had been buried. And then I overcame that pathetic ancient dryad." He picked up a silver knife and began to cut the seal. "At last I have it in my possession. And I will set him free."

Stella felt sick. There was a cold lump in her throat.

"The Grimpen Sorcerer," said the Professor reverently. "The greatest of his age. He was tricked and trapped here. But I will set him free. And he will reward me."

His face was radiant.

He drew the cork from the bottle.

Twenty-Three

For a moment, nothing happened. In the quiet, Stella could hear the wind howling around the tower.

The Professor held the bottle in both hands. It glowed in the candlelight, making flickering silver reflections on the lenses of his spectacles.

Something dark moved, just out of sight. Stella darted a look behind but saw nothing but wavering shadows.

With a sigh, like a wave breaking over a pebbly beach, a faint wisp of smoke emerged from the bottle, curled into the air, and disappeared.

Stella felt the back of her neck prickling.

Another wisp of smoke snaked from the bottle. It seemed to feel its way into the air, coiling and twisting like a serpent. The bottle glowed more brightly, with an intense silver light.

The Professor drew in a breath between his teeth. His hands were shaking and his knuckles were white. Plumes of smoke curled up into the air, thickening and swirling into vague shapes of faces and creatures and twisting figures.

Gert whispered, "Flipping heck."

Shadow hissed. The kitten gripped Ben's shoulder, her ears flat against her head and her tail as spiky as a bottle brush.

There came another sigh, like a gust of wind. Stella felt the air move. The pages of the book on the workbench fluttered. Smoke poured from the bottle, twisting into the air. It was difficult to believe so much smoke could come from such a tiny bottle. It formed a thickening column in the air above their heads. Faces appeared and opened their mouths wide. Fish swam through tendrils of weed. Strange creatures flickered and writhed and dissolved into one another.

Stella's hair blew across her face. She pushed it back. A hunched figure was forming in the smoke. It twisted its head from side to side. The sighing grew louder and became a roar, like crashing waves.

The Professor cried out and dropped the bottle onto the workbench. His fingers were white and blistered. The bottle was covered with ice crystals.

Cold wind whipped around the room. Papers flew up into the air. The candles sputtered and the fire flared wildly.

Stella spied the cork from the bottle, lying on the floor under the workbench. She looked at the Professor, but he did not see her; he was staring up at the smoke.

She crept behind him, her eyes on his back. She bent quickly and snatched up the cork. She unfolded the cuff of her coat sleeve and let the thick fabric fall over her hand.

The creature in the smoke seemed to be struggling to free itself. Its enormous head and long neck writhed and twisted.

The Professor's face was alight with hope. "Sorcerer. Hear me," he said. The figure lifted its head. Its face was still half-formed, smoky and changing. It opened its wide mouth and roared.

Stella darted around the Professor and reached for the bottle, the sleeve of her coat protecting her hand from the freezing cold. At the same time, Gert flung herself at the Professor and grasped his arm. He struggled with Gert, threw her aside with a curse, and seized Stella, but his injured hands were weak, and she twisted away from him and reached again for the bottle. He pushed her roughly away, turned the ring on his finger, and shouted, "Boy. Keep them back."

Ben grabbed Stella's arm and dragged her away from the workbench. His face was set and pale.

"Let me go," she gasped.

He took a breath, with obvious effort, and whispered, "I can't." He tried to say more, but no words came. He shook his head. His eyes were on the ring on the Professor's finger.

Then Stella understood. The Professor turned the ring on his finger each time he gave Ben an order. The ring with the dark stone. She pulled free from Ben's grasp, flung herself onto the Professor, and clutched his arm. He cursed again and struck her hard on the side of her head, but she clung on to his wrist and managed to wrench the ring from his finger.

"No!" he shouted.

She threw the ring onto the floor and stamped on it with the heavy nailed heel of her boot. It made a satisfying crunch. The stone shattered, and a few dark red drops stained the stone floor.

Ben gave a gasp and staggered. He looked

bewildered. "It's gone." He put his hands to his head. "It's gone," he said again.

"Hold her back, boy!" shouted the Professor.

Ben stepped back and stood up straight. He took a deep breath and said "No."

The Professor spoke, but his words were lost as the smoke figure roared again. They looked up. It was enormous. A tall, twisting column reaching almost to the ceiling. The face glared down at them from the shadows. Its eyes were like gas lamps, its mouth a gaping cave of teeth.

"Sorcerer. It is I, Aloysius Starke."

The Professor's voice was drowned in the rushing wind. Glass jars fell from the shelves and shattered on the floor. The candles flickered and went out.

Stella saw another chance and darted forward. The Professor lunged at her and dragged her away. She struggled free and seized the bottle. The billowing smoke filled her mouth and eyes. She coughed. She could not see. Even through the thick fabric of her coat sleeve, the bottle froze her hand. She gritted her teeth and tried to force the cork back in. The Professor clasped her around the chest, pinning her arms, and lifted her off the floor. She struggled and kicked. But he was too strong. He started to prize her fingers from the bottle.

Ben and Gert flung themselves at the Professor, making him stagger. His grip loosened. Stella wriggled free. She darted around the workbench and ducked down into a narrow space behind a tall cabinet. She crouched there, hidden, gasping, struggling to push the cork into the bottle. It was difficult; her hands were frozen and her eyes were full of smoke.

She heard scuffles and thumps. Gert cried out. Something fell and shattered.

Stella gritted her teeth, ignored the freezing ache seeping into her fingers, and forced the cork firmly into the bottle.

From the darkness above came a deafening howl. The door broke open with a crash, and the room was full of rain and wind and the sound of waves.

"No!" screamed the Professor, his voice cracking with fury. He spun around.

Stella shrank back into the shadow, desperately hoping he would not see her. She felt her head swim, as if she were fading and dissolving into the darkness. The Professor lurched toward her. She froze. His gaze seemed to focus beyond her. As if he could not see her. As if she were not there at all.

He reached for her, his fingers clutching blindly at the air. His groping hand met her neck. She felt his fingers pass through her, scrabbling against the wall, clasping only air.

He recoiled and gasped. His wide eyes stared right at her, but somehow he did not see her. She felt as if the room were spinning and she were fading away. He reached out toward her again.

Ben thumped into him. The Professor fell and struck his head on the workbench.

Ben grabbed Stella's arm and pulled her to her feet. He had a canvas bag under his arm, and he was tucking Shadow into the neck of his coat.

"We got to get away," he said.

"But—" She felt dizzy.

"Come on," said Gert.

Ben pulled her toward the door.

The smoke serpent howled again.

The Professor lurched to his feet, arms outstretched, fingers clutching the air.

Stella ducked under his grasping hands.

"Come back," he groaned. "Give it to me."

Stella pushed the silver bottle into her coat pocket and buttoned the flap as she turned and ran.

Outside, the icy wind and rain knocked the breath out of her. It was almost dawn. The sky was a leaden gray with streaks of yellow. The causeway stretched toward the shore, gleaming in the murky light.

Gert was very pale and shaking with cold. Ben pulled off his coat and helped her into it. She winced as she pushed her injured arm into the sleeve.

"We got to run," said Ben, looking out at the causeway. He held Shadow safe under his shirt with one hand; the other clutched his canvas bag under his arm. "There ain't much time. Tide's turning."

"Can you do it?" Stella put her arm around Gert.

Gert bit her lip but nodded resolutely.

They scrambled down the steps to the causeway and ran along it, over the sea. The flagstones were broken and uneven, draped with seaweed and spiked with clusters of mussel shells. Deep, dark water swirled at either side. Stella's boots slid on the wet flagstones. The rain plastered her hair to her face. The wind buffeted them. She and Gert clung together. It was difficult to keep upright.

A huge white-capped wave broke across the causeway. Water swirled around their ankles. Stella tripped and almost fell. Ben slung his bag over his shoulder and took her hand. They splashed through the icy water, slipping and stumbling.

Ahead, through the spray, Stella could see the shore, a dark blur on the horizon. Gulls sailed past, crying. The air was full of flying spray. Salt burned her throat. She coughed, choked, and gasped for air as she ran.

Another wave broke over the causeway. The swirling water reached their knees. They waded through, struggling to keep their balance. The water pulled at Stella's legs. Her boots felt as heavy as stones, and her wet clothes clung to her, weighing her down. They ran on.

Stella stopped for a moment, panting, and looked back toward the tower. She felt her insides lurch. The Professor was coming. He was on horseback, riding quickly, galloping along the causeway, a dark shape crouched low over the horse's neck. Spray flew up from the horse's hooves.

Ben looked back. "Run," he gasped.

Twenty-Four

They ran headlong, gasping for breath, splashing through water, stumbling over slippery flagstones. The shore was in sight, but behind them the sound of the horse's hooves came closer and closer.

Ben glanced over his shoulder, and his foot skidded on seaweed. He screamed as he fell off the edge of the causeway. He hit the swirling water with a huge splash and went under.

Stella and Gert flung themselves down, scraping their legs on the spiky mussel shells. Ben was struggling, swallowing water. His eyes were wide with panic. Stella grasped his slippery wet hand and hauled him back. He scrambled onto the causeway, clutching Shadow to his chest, coughing and spluttering, breath rasping. They pulled him to his feet.

"Come on," gasped Stella.

But it was too late. The Professor's horse was there, above her. It seemed enormous, stamping and blowing. The Professor leaned down and reached for her with clawing fingers. His spectacles were gone, and his eyes glinted like wet pebbles.

Another wave crashed across the causeway, almost knocking her from her feet.

The Professor clutched her arm. She struggled and managed to twist herself free.

"GIVE IT TO ME!" he screamed.

He grabbed her again.

Ben tried to pull her away.

There was a roaring, louder than the wind.

Gert yelled.

The Professor looked behind and shouted something, but Stella could not hear his words. He let go of her, raised his arms, and shouted again.

A huge wave crashed across the causeway. It lifted them off their feet and tumbled them over and over. Stella could not breathe and she could not see. She collided with a submerged rock. Desperately struggling to get her face above the surface, she managed to gulp a mouthful of air, but then she was under again. She could not feel the ground. Her lungs were bursting. She was sinking, drowning.

A huge pale shape appeared out of the darkness

below her. It swam past at tremendous speed. Stella was whirled around, swept along, and dragged across sand and shingle. Icy waves crashed and swirled. She gasped for breath and choked on salt water and smoke.

An enormous creature was in the water with her. It cut through the waves smoothly, like a gigantic fish. She had a glimpse of a vast head on a long, long neck, rising up from the water. A mouth opened above her, impossibly wide, and roared. A blast of icy smoke slammed into her. Everything was a confusion of smoke and salt water and spray. Then she was underwater again.

She fought to the surface and saw the Professor clinging to the causeway. He lifted a hand to the enormous serpent that reared above him. It roared. Then, like a striking snake, it swooped down and swallowed him.

The causeway was empty. The Professor was gone.

Stella was pulled under again. The water churned and crashed. She could not breathe. Her lungs were burning. A wave lifted her and threw her down onto sand and pebbles. She struggled through the swirling water toward the shore until she was on her hands and knees in the shallows.

Out to sea, the enormous ghostly serpent arched through the waves. It roared again.

As Stella watched, tendrils of smoke curled from its body and blew away. For a moment, she could still see the huge creature, diving through the waves, swimming away, out to sea. And then it became only silver smoke that swirled and drifted apart and dissolved into the air and was gone.

Stella was shivering with cold, frozen, dizzy, and exhausted. Her whole body was aching. She heard coughing. Gert was floundering in the water. Stella pulled herself to her feet and staggered back into the sea to help her. They stumbled onto the shore, away from the crashing waves, panting and shivering.

"Look," said Gert.

Farther along the beach lay a dark shape. They hurried over. Ben was on his back, his face white, his eyes closed. There was a nasty-looking purplish graze on his forehead. Shadow mewed anxiously and pawed at his closed eyes.

"Ben?" said Stella.

He did not answer. She touched his face. He stirred and muttered something. His skin was cold. She shook him.

"Wake up."

He opened his eyes, said "What?" and shut them again.

"Come on," she said. "We have to go and get help."

His eyes fluttered open, and he looked at her without recognition.

"It's me, Stella," she said. "And Gert."

"Stella."

They took his arms and pulled him to his feet. He staggered and bent over, his hands on his knees.

"You all right?" asked Gert, patting his back.

"Can you walk?" asked Stella.

"Reckon," he said, and stood up shakily. He staggered again. "Maybe."

Shadow climbed up onto Ben's shoulder. She made some encouraging chirruping noises and bit him on the ear.

Stella took Ben's sodden canvas bag and slung it over her shoulder. She felt in her pocket. The silver bottle was still there. She looked about, shielding her eyes from the rain. It was almost daylight. The causeway was nearly underwater again. Farther out to sea, waves crashed around the island, throwing spray into the air.

They had to find shelter. But where? "Come on," she said. She took Ben's arm.

The wind felt like ice. They trudged along the beach, leaning against one another, wet through and shivering. Ben's eyes were closed. He stumbled. Stella put her arm around him. "Stay awake," she said.

Her wet hair blew across her face. She pushed it back and blinked the rain out of her eyes.

Farther along the beach, a figure was approaching.

Stella tried to call out, but her head was so light it felt as if it were floating, and only a croak came out of her throat.

The figure was waving. Small shapes circled it, separate and flickering.

Stella tried to call again.

She heard someone shout, and she could see the figure coming closer, but it seemed enormously far away and spinning strangely.

Then there was darkness.

Twenty-Five

Stella swam up out of a dream and heard music. She opened her eyes. She was lying in a narrow bunk bed, covered with blankets, in a tiny room. A hot brick was against her feet. The music came from somewhere nearby. It sounded familiar, like a steam organ with many wheezing, wailing pipes. She swallowed. Her mouth tasted of orange peel and herbs.

She sat up and looked around, feeling bewildered and dizzy. The room was full of dark wood and shining brass. There were two bunk beds, one above the other. The ceiling was curved and painted with leaves and flowers. Copper pans dangled from hooks overhead. A small stove surrounded with rose-patterned tiles stood under a carved mantelpiece. Wire cages and woven baskets were piled in a corner. Weak sunlight slanted in through a small window.

Where was she? She felt for the silver bottle in the pocket of her coat, but the coat was gone. She was wearing a linen nightshirt, much too large for her. Where were her clothes? Where was the silver bottle? And where were Gert and Ben?

She climbed stiffly out of the bunk bed. Everything ached. She went to the window and looked out. Shingle sloped toward the sea. Not far away, a seagull glared at her from a large rock. In the distance, sunshine sparkled on white-flecked waves around the island.

She tiptoed across the room to the door and opened it silently. Stepping outside, shading her eyes against the daylight, she halted, astonished. She was at the doorway of a beautiful wagon parked on the shingle. Three steps led down to the ground. She climbed down. The wagon was painted red and blue and gold, and on the side, in curling gold letters, was written,

SIGNOR
CAPELLI'S
EDUCATED CATS
Astonishing
Performances

Nearby, a large driftwood fire was burning. Clothes on a line flapped in the breeze. Two horses cropped the spiky grass that grew beside the seashore.

Mr. Capelli was standing by the fire, playing his violin. His seven cats were perched around him on stones, and they were singing. Ben and Gert sat beside the fire, wrapped in blankets, eating soup. Shadow was perched on Ben's shoulder, watching the other cats. She made an experimental squeaking mew and Mr. Capelli smiled at her, nodded, and said, "*Sì, sì* little one. Most beautiful."

Ben looked up, saw Stella standing beside the wagon, and grinned.

Gert waved a spoon at her. She said, "You're up."

Mr. Capelli stopped playing and turned around. "Stella Montgomery," he said. "It is most splendid to see you again." He laid down his violin and bustled over to her. "You are well? Your head? Your heart? Your limbs? You are not entirely frozen?"

"Yes—I mean no. Thank you. But—"

Alfredo trotted toward her with his tail pointing straight up. She bent and patted him. Several more cats came and twined around her legs. She stroked them all.

"Here." Mr. Capelli wrapped a red blanket around her shoulders and guided her toward the fire.

"Sit here," said Gert, patting a stone between her and Ben.

"You will have some fish soup?" Mr. Capelli ladled soup into a bowl from a steaming pot beside the fire and pushed it into her hands.

"Thank you, Mr. Capelli," said Stella. "But how—"

"He followed the Professor," said Gert.

"Yes, yes," said Mr. Capelli, nodding and waving the ladle emphatically. "That is true. Yesterday I saw you on the stage with the Professor. That boy is the little Stella Montgomery, I thought. I was most astonished. And then he put you in that box and you disappeared. I could not find you. I tried to talk to the police, but they would not understand me. They would not listen. And so I watched the Professor and I followed him here, late at night, all the way over the marsh. But it was dark and the weather was most dreadful. Such a storm! I lost him. So I waited here until morning. And then I saw you there on the beach."

"You were cold as a codfish," said Gert, with a giggle. "We rubbed you down and wrapped you up and Mr. Capelli shoved tonic down your throat and we put you to bed."

Stella swallowed a mouthful of soup. It was hot and salty and delicious. She was extremely hungry.

She took another spoonful and said, "How are you? Are you all right?"

"Look," said Gert. She showed Stella a bandage on her shoulder and flexed her arm. "Mr. Capelli fixed me up, right and tight."

"Does it hurt?" asked Stella.

"Not a skitch," said Gert.

Stella turned to Ben.

"I'm prime too," he said with a grin. On his shoulder, Shadow made a high-pitched squeaking noise and bit his ear. He stroked her head with his finger.

"And the Professor?" Stella asked.

"Gone. Drowned," said Gert. "That's his horse there." She pointed.

"Not drowned," said Ben definitely. "Ate up."

Then Stella remembered seeing the enormous serpent sweep down and swallow the Professor. "Yes. I saw it," she said, nodding. "I saw it eat him." She looked out at the pale sunlight sparkling on the little waves, and shuddered. "It was terrible." After a moment she said to Ben, "Well. He can't make you scry anymore."

"Nope. That's gone. Thank cripes." Ben rubbed his nose with the back of his hand. "He pricked my finger and got some blood, and he put it in that ring. So I had to do what he said. He was right there in my head, making me do things. I could feel him here." He pointed at his forehead. "It was horrible." Ben looked at her. Stella noticed again his peculiar pale gray eyes.

"You've changed," she said.

He nodded and grinned. "Reckon. When you smashed the ring, I felt him let go of me. It was good, that." He said, awkwardly, "Thank you."

Stella felt her cheeks redden. She looked at the fire. "And Mr. Filbert's bottle?" she asked.

"It is safe. It is here," said Mr. Capelli, nodding vigorously. He climbed into the wagon and appeared a moment later holding something in both hands, gingerly, as if it might explode. He passed it to Stella. It was wrapped in a tea towel. She unfolded it. The silver bottle glinted in the sunlight. She picked it up and peered into it. Inside, something small and pale seemed to twist and uncurl. She shook the bottle gently. There was a faint whispering sound, like a distant trickle of water.

"There's still something in here," she said. She pushed the cork in more firmly with her thumb.

Ben nodded. "Part of the serpent. It didn't all get out. That's why it was still just smoke, I reckon. Not real. If you ain't shoved the cork in like that, it would've got right out, and it would be swimming around now, making storms and eating people."

Stella shivered again, remembering the monstrous ghostly serpent. She wrapped the cloth carefully back around the bottle.

"It stayed long enough to eat the Professor," said Ben. "Then it just blew away. Professor thought when he opened the bottle, the sorcerer would hop out and reward him. But it was the serpent instead."

Stella said, "What do you mean?"

"It was the Grimpen Sorcerer. Professor was always on about the story."

"So, who was the Grimpen Sorcerer?" asked Stella.

"What story? Tell us the story," said Gert.

Mr. Capelli moved closer. "Yes, yes," he said. His cats sat up straight and looked attentive.

"Well," said Ben, looking around at them. "It's from long ago. Ages ago. The Grimpen Sorcerer. He built that castle." He pointed out to sea, to the island. "It's ruined now, but before, it had turrets and a seawall. Professor showed me a picture of it. It was much bigger then. A proper castle. And the Grimpen Sorcerer lived there. He could do magic, all kinds. Change into a bird or a fish, and make the weather. That was proper magic, in the old days. Real magic."

He paused and looked doubtfully at them, as if unsure of their interest. They all nodded, and Gert said, "Go on."

Ben continued, with more confidence, "Well, at first he helped people. Making it rain for the farmers, finding sheep and that. But it wasn't enough for him, he was full of magic and very proud. And he wanted gold. But the people were skint, living on the marsh there, and they couldn't pay him. They only had seaweed and fish guts, I reckon. And so he got angry, and then he turned into a serpent and he raised a storm and a huge big wave flooded the marsh. And one village went right under and people drowned.

"And so then the villagers wanted to kill the serpent. But when they chopped a bit off him, it just grew back. And even angrier than before. And so they tricked him. They tricked him into changing shape. Into a bear, and then a wolf and then an eagle. And then they said, What about a tiny creature? Reckon you can't do that. And he changed into a worm. And they trapped the worm in the little bottle. And then they buried the bottle under the magic tree, so it would be safe hidden. They reckoned that was the end of him."

"But that's just a story people tell little kids. A fairy tale," said Gert, after a moment. "It's not real."

Ben nodded. "That's what everyone reckons. But the Professor thought different. So he read that old book, and he found where the bottle was hidden. He thought he'd open the bottle and the Grimpen Sorcerer would just hop out and give him a reward. Teach him some magic, maybe. That's what he wanted. But the sorcerer came out as the serpent. And even more angry, being stuck in that bottle so long. And so the Professor got ate up."

There was quiet for a few moments. Stella watched the blue flames flicker and crackle on the driftwood. She thought about the Professor. He had done some terrible things, and he had killed poor Mr. Filbert. But she remembered his face, alight with hope as he opened the bottle. And then terrified, clinging to the causeway as the serpent swept down on him. It must have been horrible to be eaten like that.

"I do feel sorry for him," she said.

"I don't," said Ben.

"Me neither," said Gert. She rubbed her bandaged shoulder. "Serves him flipping well right."

Twenty-Six

The fire crackled, the cats sang, and the clothes on the line flapped in the breeze. On Ben's shoulder, Shadow was alert, watching the other cats with her head on one side. She made some piercing squeaks. Ben grinned and stroked her.

Stella put down her bowl and wrapped her arms around herself, listening to the music and watching the seagulls sailing past on the wind. Sunshine sparkled on the sea. White-capped waves broke around the island.

All at once, she remembered that moment when she had tried to hide, crouched behind the cabinet, and the Professor had reached out toward her and his fingers had passed right though her, as if she were not there at all. She shivered, remembering the confusing, dizzy feeling of fading and falling away. Like a lump of sugar dissolving in a cup of tea.

Under the blanket, she squeezed the bones in her elbows. They felt reassuringly solid and familiar. Surely it was not possible to disappear like that? Could she have imagined it? She wanted to ask Ben or Gert or Mr. Capelli about it, but she was not sure she wanted to hear the answer. What if she was something horrible, like the worm in Mr. Filbert's bottle?

She swallowed and shook her head, trying to lose the disconcerting feeling that she was no longer exactly herself.

The music ended. Mr. Capelli laid his violin down and stroked his cats, saying something to each of them. To Shadow he said, "Very good, little one. You have talent."

Ben grinned. Shadow bit him on his ear.

"So you are recovered? You are all quite well now?" said Mr. Capelli.

They all nodded.

"You will return to your Aunts?" Mr. Capelli asked Stella. "They will be most frightfully deranged. And the police are searching for you."

"Yes," she said, with a sinking feeling in her insides. The Aunts would be extremely angry. But surely, even at their most furious, they could not be more frightening than the Professor and the Grimpen Serpent. She straightened her shoulders and said, "Yes. I will go back to my Aunts."

Mr. Capelli turned to Gert. "And you will return to Mrs. MacTaggerty?'

Gert nodded. "Of course. She'll be having kittens."

"What about you?" Mr. Capelli asked Ben. "Where will you go?"

Ben shrugged. He stroked Shadow and said, "We'll be all right."

"You will perhaps come and work with me? As my apprentice? My cats like you. The little one has most splendid talent, and we are in need of a soprano voice."

Ben looked at him for a moment.

"That's a prime offer," said Gert professionally.

Ben hesitated, and then nodded and said, "Yes. Yes, please."

Mr. Capelli beamed. He leaned down and shook Ben's hand. "That is most splendid," he said. "We will work together. My cats will become even more famous. We will travel the world."

Ben grinned and stroked Shadow. She bit his hand hard and then made a noise like a whistling kettle.

Mr. Capelli felt the clothes on the line. "They are

almost dry. Good. Because we must go, right now, straightaway. We must cross the marsh before dark."

"How far is it to Withering-by-Sea?" asked Stella.

"Ten miles, perhaps more."

Stella and Gert dressed inside the wagon. Gert's yellow dancing dress was limp and torn, and most of the spangles were gone.

"Mrs. Mac'll have a flipping fit when she sees this," said Gert with a giggle. Her dancing shoes had been lost in the sea, and so she had borrowed an old pair of Mr. Capelli's boots. They were much too large for her. She did a couple of comical, clumping dance steps in them and twirled around.

Stella pulled on her shirt and coat and trousers. They were even more ragged than before, and stiff with salt. Gert helped comb her hair. It was so knotted and tangled that it broke several teeth on Mr. Capelli's comb. Gert tied it back with a piece of string. Then Stella combed Gert's hair as well as she could.

"Your ringlets are all gone," she said.

"They ain't natural, girl," said Gert. "Mrs. Mac does 'em with a hot poker."

Stella picked up the silver bottle and tucked it into the pocket of her coat.

"What are you going to do with that?" asked Gert

as she wrapped a blanket around Stella's shoulders.

"I don't know," said Stella. She remembered Mr. Filbert. *Keep it safe,* he had said. She buttoned the flap of the pocket.

Mr. Capelli took the cats' cages from the wagon. The cats were very reluctant to be caught. When they saw the cages they hissed, puffed up their tails, arched their backs, and dashed about. Mr. Capelli flapped his arms and called encouragingly to them in several languages.

Ben tucked Shadow safely away into the neck of his coat and caught Giorgio and Flora and Alfredo, one by one. He stroked them and spoke softly to them to calm them. As he put them in their cages, Mr. Capelli said, "Yes, my cats like you. That is splendid."

Gert caught Gastone. Stella managed to corner Annina beneath the wagon, clasp her around her middle, and drag her out. Giuseppi and Violetta climbed up onto the roof of the wagon and had to be tempted down with the remains of the fish soup.

At last, when all seven cats were in their cages, inside the wagon (and Stella, Ben, and Gert were covered with cat fur and Stella had been scratched several times), Mr. Capelli harnessed his shaggy cart horse to the wagon, hitched the Professor's horse behind, then climbed up and took the reins.

Ben helped Gert and Stella scramble up onto the wide bench at the front of the wagon beside Mr. Capelli. Ben began to follow them, then gave a sudden start and clapped his hand to his head.

"I forgot," he said, and jumped back to the ground.

"What?"

He didn't answer. He dashed over to where his canvas bag was lying on the shingle. He picked it up and hurried back to the wagon.

"I forgot," he said again, and he stopped and rummaged inside. "Here it is." He pulled something out of the bag and handed it up to Stella.

She gasped. It was the Atlas. Wet, salt-stained, and battered. She took it from him with trembling hands.

"Saw you drop it in the theater," he said. "So I nabbed it for you."

"Thank you," she whispered. She felt her eyes prickle with tears. She had thought she would never see it again. She stroked its familiar cover and hugged it to her chest. Ben climbed up beside her. Mr. Capelli clicked his tongue to the horse, and the wagon began to move.

"Thank you," Stella said again to Ben as the wagon jolted over the sand and shingle toward the road.

"That's all right," he said.

The road curved away from the coast. They soon left the sound of the sea behind. The marsh stretched away to the horizon. The road was on an embankment, several feet above the boggy ground. Pools of water reflected the hazy sky and little birds twittered, unseen, in the tall reeds. Mr. Capelli hummed to himself and occasionally sang a snatch of something. Gert's boots thumped on the footboard in time to the music. Shadow purred and made little chirruping noises through the open window to the other cats inside the wagon.

Stella laid the Atlas on her lap and patted it. The little twig was still in place. She took it out carefully from under the ribbon. The tiny leaves were limp and battered, but still green.

"What's that?" asked Ben.

Stella showed him the twig. "I think—" she started to say. "I mean—it's a bit of Mr. Filbert." She looked into Ben's puzzled face. "The gentleman at the hotel. The one that the Professor stabbed."

Ben gently touched the tiny green leaves. He said, "A bit of him?"

Stella told him how Mr. Filbert had turned into sticks, and how she had found the little twig in his hand.

"Nobble me granny," said Gert.

Ben said slowly, "When we was cutting down that old tree, here on the marsh, he come out of nowhere, in the dark, and grabbed that bottle and scarpered."

"He was the spirit of the tree. A dryad. That's why they buried the bottle there," said Stella. "Because they knew he would protect it. And he woke up when you cut the tree down. He only wanted to keep the bottle safe."

Gert said, "He must've been very old, if he was as old as a tree."

Stella remembered Mr. Filbert and how ancient he had seemed. "Perhaps that's why he went to the hotel. To drink the water. It's healthy for old people. It's famous."

She untied the ribbon from the Atlas, using her fingers and then her teeth to loosen the knot. She opened it and peeled apart the damp pages. It was lovely to see the familiar pictures again. An elephant with an elaborate canopied tent on its back, a curved iron bridge carrying a train over a canyon, an enormous, many-toothed crocodile lying half-submerged in a swamp.

At last she found the page she was looking for. A long, curving coastline sprinkled with towns. She showed Ben with her finger. "Look. Here we are."

In the Atlas, the marsh that stretched away on all sides of the wagon was no bigger than a visiting card.

"Here's the island." She pointed. The causeway was a tiny dotted line jutting out into the sea. The island was a green speck the size of a pinhead. "This is Withering-by-Sea, here." She pointed to a dot at the edge of the marsh and read out, "'The healthful mineral waters of the area have been known since ancient times and are beneficial to all Rheumatic, Gouty, and Hysterical Afflictions and every Disease accompanied by Debility or Great Age.'"

Ben looked at the map with interest. He said, "It's everything, isn't it? Just small."

Stella nodded. "It's got the whole world in it." She passed the Atlas over to him. He laid it on his lap and traced the road through the marsh with his finger.

"Look," he said, pointing.

The map was blotched with mildew and salt water, but Stella could just see an indistinct winding line leading from the road and ending at a tiny dot, somewhere in the middle of the marsh.

"I reckon it's that village that got drowned," said Ben. "Where we cut down that tree."

"Is it?" asked Stella doubtfully.

He looked at her with his serious gray eyes and nodded.

Stella turned the little twig over between her fingers. "Could we plant it there, do you think, Mr. Capelli? Where Mr. Filbert lived?"

Ben traced his finger along the map. "It's not too far from the road," he said. "I remember this track. It's hard to see, but with the map, I reckon I can find it again."

Mr. Capelli looked at the map and then at the sun, which was sinking slowly in the sky, and said, "Yes, yes. If there is time. That is most splendid."

Stella put the little twig into her pocket with the silver bottle and carefully buttoned the flap.

The wagon rolled on through the marsh. Here and there were rocky outcrops and groups of wintry trees. Low hills rose like islands above the pools of water.

Ben watched the marsh intently, his finger on the map. Tendrils of mist drifted across the road. The horizon was lost in a grayish haze. He said, "It's not far now, I reckon," and a few minutes later, he said, "There," and pointed. A faint track snaked away from the road and disappeared into the mist. It was winding, overgrown, and half-submerged in the marsh.

Mr. Capelli asked, doubtfully, "You are sure? It would be most dreadful if we become lost."

"I'm dead sure," said Ben. "I remember it."

Mr. Capelli glanced at him for a moment, then nodded, flicked the reins, and turned the wagon. They jolted down the embankment. The narrow track wound away from the road, uneven and boggy. The wagon lurched as it splashed through puddles. Stella braced her boots against the footboard.

Mist was coming in from the sea. The air tasted like salt. The wagon continued on slowly. They passed a group of stunted trees. Their bare branches made a jagged pattern against the hazy sky, fading into the mist like a wet ink drawing.

Stella remembered a frightening story Polly had told her, of a coach and four horses that had left the road through the marsh, had driven into a slough, and had been sucked under and never seen again.

It was very cold. She pulled the blanket more tightly around her shoulders as the wagon trundled farther away from the road and into the mist.

Twenty-Seven

The wagon jolted along through the marsh. The track curved around the side of a low hill and then down between tall reeds and through shallow, muddy puddles. The drifting mist made it difficult to see far ahead. Sometimes the path seemed to disappear altogether, and Mr. Capelli slowed the horse, and they went on cautiously through the reeds until they found their way again.

Stella stared into the swirling mist, watching indistinct shapes emerge and then vanish again. A pile of stones covered with moss. A fallen branch sprouting lichen and fungus, orange and yellow and white. Twisted, wintry trees wound around with ivy and mistletoe.

A distant booming cry echoed across the marsh, throbbing and dying away.

"Cripes," whispered Gert. "What was that?"

"A *tarabuso,*" said Mr. Capelli reassuringly. "A bittern. A bird, only."

"It's right creepy out here," said Gert, her voice shaking a bit.

"It ain't far now," said Ben.

They came across a mossy wall that followed the track for a short distance, and then disappeared into the water, a tumble of broken stones. Then they passed a cottage, half-sunk in the marsh, covered in moss and ivy. Beyond were piles of broken stones and a second cottage, its windows empty and dark and fringed with tiny ferns. Farther on were more houses, some of them only moss-covered mounds.

A ruined church tower loomed out of the mist. A tree grew inside the church. Its branches stuck out through the empty windows and the holes in the roof. In the churchyard, stone angels lay amongst toppled gravestones covered with moss. Ferns grew everywhere. Thickets of ancient holly and yew twisted together, entangled with ivy.

"I remember this," whispered Ben. "We walked from here."

Mr. Capelli clucked to the horse and drew the wagon to a halt. Beside the road, a row of tumbledown houses huddled together. Beyond, more cottages were only indistinct shapes in the mist. It was very quiet and very cold.

Stella imagined there were voices in the silence, just beyond hearing. She turned to look, but the village was silent and still. The dark, empty windows of the houses stared back at her.

They climbed down from the wagon. The ground was extremely boggy. Water soaked into Stella's boots. Despite the blanket, she shivered.

Mr. Capelli spoke to the horses and the cats and shuttered the windows on the wagon.

"It's this way," said Ben. He led them through the drowned village.

Stella tried to walk on the firmer parts of the ground, grass tussocks and patches of moss, but her boot went unexpectedly into a pool of black mud. She pulled it out with a revolting sucking sound. It seemed very loud in the silence.

Gert giggled, then put a hand over her mouth.

Ben led them past the churchyard and along a narrow, fern-lined passage between two houses, to the edge of the village. They passed a water mill, sunk into the marsh. Its wheel was crooked and rotten and draped with slime.

Water dripped slowly into a stagnant green pond. Beyond the mill, they pushed through a tangle of brambles and twisted trees that clung to the side of a low hill. Mossy stone steps led upward. They climbed the steps to a ruined stone wall and passed through an archway into an overgrown garden. Moss grew thickly between broken flagstones. Ivy tangled in amongst the trees.

It was very still.

Ben pushed his way in, through the thicket of holly and ivy. Stella and Gert and Mr. Capelli followed gingerly. They reached a clearing and stopped at the edge of a gaping dark hole. An ancient tree lay cut down, its roots curled high into the air. Its mossy branches were gnarled and twisted and broken. Its few remaining dry leaves made a faint whispering sound, although there was no breeze.

Stella felt tears stinging her eyes. She laid her hand on the tree. The bark felt smooth under her fingers.

Ben touched the tree sadly. "It was horrible out here that night."

Shadow, tucked into the neck of his coat, made a small squeak.

Stella imagined the drowned village in the dark. The Professor and his men cutting down the tree by lantern light and digging up the roots. And Mr. Filbert, wrenched from his long sleep, appearing suddenly from the heart of the fallen tree, snatching the little bottle, and fleeing across the marsh. Desperate to keep it safe.

She felt a cold ache in her heart. The tree must have stood here, on this hill in the little village, for many, many years. People had entrusted their secrets to it. But the village had been drowned and abandoned. And the tree had become old and overgrown. And now it was dead.

She blinked back her tears, looked around the clearing, and found a patch of moss in a sheltered corner beside a huge stone. She crouched down and dug with her fingers in the ground. The earth was soft and dark. It did not take long to dig a hole. She took the little bottle from her pocket, laid it in the hole, and covered it up.

Then she carefully planted the hazel twig above the bottle and pushed earth around it. The twig would grow into a tree and protect its secret. The silver bottle would be safe.

She stood up and rubbed her eyes with her sleeve.

Gert nodded. "That's prime," she said.

"Yes," said Mr. Capelli. He made a flickering

gesture with his hand to his forehead and his heart, and bowed his head.

"Good-bye, Mr. Filbert," whispered Stella.

Ben held Shadow against his chest and mumbled something that Stella did not hear.

They stood in silence for a moment. Then they turned away from the fallen tree and went back through the thicket and the archway in the wall and down the hill to the empty village.

Just as they reached the church, the mist parted and a shaft of weak sunshine shone through. It fell on the moss and the curling ferns, and all at once, every tiny water droplet caught the light and twinkled. The drowned village sparkled, as if it were scattered with diamonds. It was quite beautiful.

Again Stella imagined she could almost hear voices, this time laughing and singing. Just beyond hearing, just out of reach. She held her breath. For a moment the village sparkled and the silent music swirled. Then the mist closed in again, and the drowned cottages were lost to view.

Stella breathed again.

"Cripes," said Gert. "That was like magic."

"*Gran Dio*," whispered Mr. Capelli.

Ben grinned at Stella but did not say anything.

Beyond the church, the wagon was a cheerful red

and blue and gold shape in the mist. The cats yowled a welcome, and Shadow squeaked in reply.

Mr. Capelli patted the horse's neck, climbed up, and took the reins.

"And now, we go home," he said.

Twenty-Eight

They found the road again without any trouble. The wagon rolled on toward Withering-by-Sea, through the drizzling rain and fading light. Mr. Capelli hummed to himself, and inside the wagon the cats chirruped and mewed. Shadow made an occasional earsplitting squeak. Stella sat between Gert and Ben, wrapped in a blanket, warm and safe and extremely muddy.

The drizzle was becoming heavier. Reluctantly Ben put the pages of the Atlas back into a tidy pile. As he closed it, something fluttered out. Stella bent and picked it up from the footboard. She had forgotten about the photograph. It was damp and blotched with seawater, but still clear.

Gert said, "What's that?"

"It's that photograph I found," said Stella. "What

do you think? Is that me?" She passed the photograph to Gert, who studied it with her head on one side.

"Could be you," she said. "You've got the same eyes. But there's two of you. Twins, looks like. Is that really your ma there, do you think?"

"I don't know," said Stella.

"You need to ask those Aunts of yours," said Gert. "Something odd going on with you, girl. Something secret."

Stella imagined the secret lurking inside her chest. Curling and uncurling in the dark. She looked at the three faces in the photograph. They stared back at her, wide-eyed. She remembered again the strange moment on the island. When it felt as if she had faded away and disappeared and the Professor's clutching hand had passed right through her.

Like being lost in the mist. But truly lost. Lost and gone.

She took a breath and said, "You remember, on the island? With the Professor? Did I—I mean—Did you see—?" She stopped. She found she couldn't ask, *Did you see me disappear?* But she wanted to know.

Ben said, "I always knew you was fey." He looked at her and nodded. "First time I seen you."

"So I did—I did—"

He nodded again. "Yes. It was like you were there, but not there."

"You couldn't see me?"

"Nope. Just for a second or two. But I knew you was there, and when I grabbed your arm, I saw you again."

Stella said, "It felt so strange."

"Was that the first time?" he asked.

She nodded. "Yes, of course." But then she thought of the many times she had hidden from Ada and the Aunts. She had always been extremely good at hiding. At being overlooked. She remembered that night in the conservatory, when she had been hiding from the Professor's men, and she was certain Scuttler would see her, but his eyes had slid over her. As if she had become part of the shadow.

"Maybe," she said thoughtfully. She remembered again what Aunt Condolence had said. *Disgraceful, even for a half—* And she had stopped. A half what? Who was she? The Aunts knew, and they did not want to tell her. She looked at the photograph again. Then she pushed it into her pocket and buttoned the flap. "I'll find out," she said. "If they won't answer my questions, I'll find out another way."

Gert nodded. "That's flipping right, girl," she said. "You do that."

It was dusk when they reached Withering-by-Sea, and the lights along the Front were twinkling in the drizzle. On the pier, the steam organ played and the merry-go-round twirled and sparkled.

As they drove along the Front, a little boy came running up beside the wagon. He shrieked, "It's her! It's Gert! Mrs. Mac! Mrs. Mac!" and sped away toward the pier, waving his arms and yelling. Farther away along the Front, someone looked up, pointed, and shouted something. Out on the pier, a man waved and began to run toward the theater.

By the time they reached the pier, children were skipping beside the wagon, calling out and laughing, and a crowd had gathered. Mr. Capelli clucked to the horse, the wagon lurched to a halt near the turnstiles, and they all scrambled down.

The Fairy Bells, a shoal of small, sparkly figures, tumbled through the turnstiles and darted through the crowd. They surrounded Gert, hugged her, and jumped up and down.

"You're back!"

"Where were you?"

"What happened?"

"Mrs. Mac's flipping beside herself."

They hugged Gert some more and giggled and spun her around.

"The coppers were here."

"Everyone was that upset."

"We was up all night."

A large woman pushed her way through the excited girls. She grabbed Gert and hugged her hard. She held her out at arm's length, looked at her, gave her a vigorous shake, and then hugged her again.

"Where were you, girl? Frit me half to death."

"The Professor snatched us, Mrs. Mac," said Gert. "Mr. Capelli brought us back."

Mrs. MacTaggerty gave Gert another hug and then turned and grabbed the surprised Mr. Capelli and embraced him, too. "Thank you," she said, tears rolling down her face. "Thank you for bringing her back."

"It was nothing, madam," said Mr. Capelli when he got his breath back. He straightened his hat. "It was less than nothing."

Mrs. MacTaggerty hugged him again, making him gasp. Then she hugged Stella, and then Ben, which made Shadow puff up like a porcupine and hiss. Then she hugged Mr. Capelli once more.

"Thank you," she said again, still crying. She wiped her eyes, and blew her nose on a lace-edged handkerchief.

People were all talking at once. A tall man with a magnificent curly mustache said something in a foreign language, and a woman with tattoos all over her bare arms slapped his shoulder and laughed. Someone patted Stella on her back. Two of the Fairy Bells (Ettie and one of the Marys, Stella thought) grabbed her hands and swung her around in a circle. Then Gert and two or three more girls joined them and, arm in arm, they whirled around until they were breathless and giggling.

Gert gave Stella a hug. "I didn't think we'd make it back," she said. "When we were locked up in that tower, I thought we were done for. And then I thought we'd drown in the sea, for sure. It's flippin' good to be home." She hugged Stella again, grinning.

Mr. Capelli said, "Stella Montgomery. We must go. Your Aunts will be most frightfully worried. And the police are still searching for you. We cannot waste time. I must deliver you home."

Gert said, "Thank you, Mr. Capelli," and shook his hand. She gave Ben a quick hug. "I'll see you around, boy." She wrapped her arms around Stella again and squeezed her tightly. "Good-bye, girl. Good luck," she said.

"Good-bye, Gert," said Stella. She bit her lip. She was determined not to cry. She turned away and climbed back up onto the wagon, beside Ben.

"Good-bye, good-bye," Gert and all the Fairy Bells shouted, waving their arms and jumping up and down. Mrs. MacTaggerty wiped her eyes again and waved her handkerchief.

Stella swallowed the lump in her throat, smiled as well as she could, and waved.

Mr. Capelli clucked to the horse and flicked the reins, and the wagon started to move. They drove away from the pier along the Front, away from the music and the happy crowd, past the pleasure gardens and the smaller hotels, and then began to climb the hill, toward the Hotel Majestic.

Stella looked up at it. All its windows were glowing. It looked like an enormous lantern.

They turned into the drive of the hotel, and Mr. Capelli drew the wagon to a stop. Stella took a deep breath. She was home. She could feel tears prickling her eyes, and she blinked them away.

"Good-bye, Mr. Capelli." She hugged him tightly. "Thank you so much for everything."

"Good-bye, Stella Montgomery," he said. "Good fortune."

She leaned through the window into the wagon and said good-bye to the cats, one by one.

Then she turned to Ben. "Good-bye. Good luck,"

she said. She stroked Shadow's head. "Good-bye, Shadow." Shadow purred and rubbed her chin against Stella's fingers.

Ben said, "Good-bye, Stella."

She gave the Atlas a last hug and passed it to him. "Here," she said. "This is for you."

He looked startled. He held it carefully, as if it were very precious. "Are you sure? Don't you want it?"

She shook her head. "I know it by heart. I don't need it anymore." She climbed down from the wagon and looked up at him. "And I want you to have it. You will need it. You're going to see the world."

She waved good-bye.

"And I'm going to find out who I am," she said.

Sounds were coming from inside the hotel. A murmur of voices. A booming echo and a birdlike twittering. Perhaps Aunt Deliverance was shouting at Aunt Temperance. A twang and a creak that sounded like Aunt Condolence's Particular Patent Corset.

Stella hesitated for a moment.

She waved for the last time.

Then she turned and walked up the steps to the front door of the hotel.

Acknowledgments

I'd like to thank Suzanne, Hazel, and Jane for reading parts of the manuscript and for their encouragement, all the lovely people at ABC Books, especially Tegan, Chren, and Kate, the May Gibbs Children's Literature Trust, and my agent, Jill Corcoran.